YAKUZA PERFUME

Other books by Blue Moon *Authors*

RICHARD MANTON

DREAM BOAT
LA VIE PARISIENNE
SWEET DREAMS
LOVE LESSONS
BELLE SAUVAGE
PEARLS OF THE ORIENT
BOMBAY BOUND

DANIEL VIAN

BLUE TANGO
SABINE
CAROUSEL
ADAGIO
BERLIN 1923

AKAHIGE NAMBAN

CHRYSANTHEMUM, ROSE, AND THE SAMURAI
SHOGUN'S AGENTS
WOMEN OF THE MOUNTAIN
WARRIORS OF THE TOWN
WOMEN OF GION

BLUE MOON BOOKS
61 Fourth Avenue
New York, New York 10003

The Victorian Era

YAKUZA PERFUME

Akahige Namban

BLUE MOON

BLUE MOON BOOKS, INC. NEW YORK

First Blue Moon Edition 1992
First Printing 1992

ISBN 0-929654-85-4

Manufactured in the United States of America

Published by Blue Moon Books, Inc.
61 Fourth Avenue
New York, New York 10003

CHAPTER 1

UNIFORM PRESENCE

The apartment smelled stale, the noise from the streets was harsh, the smoggy sunlight murky, yet it was good to be home. Jim Suzuki threw open the window and stood for a moment staring down at the street. Below him the shops were decorated with the first signs of spring. Masses of humanity pushed along the covered sidewalks or on the streets themselves. The hive that is Tokyo came rushing back through the window as he drew a deep breath.

He was of medium height and build. A slight epicanthic fold over his dark eyes, a sallow skin, dark hair betrayed traces of Oriental ancestry. He had grown older in the previous two weeks, as he had discovered more about himself and his antecedents.

"Hey, quit mooning out the window and lend a hand here."

Jim turned to survey his double. Andy Middler was the same height and build as Jim. He had brown wavy hair and a paler complexion than Jim's. His eye's were rounder. Otherwise the hawk nose and high cheekbones could have come from the same mold. Which in fact they had. Jim walked over the springy *tatami* mat. It gave under his weight. They put the bags of groceries into the tiny kitchen, then sat down to sort their mail. A two-week vacation, illuminating and sometimes even pleasant as this one had been, necessitated some adjustments upon return. Household routine took over.

Jim was at his computer, catching up on the latest news. Andy was reading his financial papers when the doorbell rang. The sound did not penetrate Jim's consciousness until he felt Andy's nudge. He looked up from the glowing screen, heard the doorbell, and blanched. Then his pulse slowed and he grinned at his brother.

"Still nervous? I thought we had settled the paternity question by now . . ."

The tension in Andy's face drained away and he grinned weakly back. "Reflexes, old son. Just me nerves." Still he made no move towards the door and Jim rose.

"Let's go and see who then."

The door opened onto the darkened corridor that framed two uniformed figures. For a brief moment Andy's pulse leaped with fear again. Having been hunted several times in the past two weeks, he found his nervous system still prone to react strongly at the sight of any unusual occurrence. Then his hindbrain recognized the figures that filled the uniforms and two parts of his anatomy reacted. His lips smiled automatically, and the bulge at his crotch started to swell.

His brother Jim pushed by Andy's still figure. "Michiko-chan! And . . . I remember you! The tour guide!" he moved aside grandiosely inviting them into the small apartment.

"Someya Hana," the tour-guide said in a low voice as she stepped forward reluctantly. Michiko Teraoka, the young neighborhood policewoman pushed forward confidently, stepping out of her shoes. There was a glint of anticipation on her broad peasant face.

The four of them seated themselves comfortably on the *tatami*. Andy looked at Hana "I'm please to see you here," he said sincerely, stroking her trembling hand. "But I didn't think you came to Tokyo . . ."

Michiko looked on with a hint of jealousy, and her own

hand stole under the otable to Jim's knee. He reciprocated with a wink as his own hand moved her palm up the leg of his trousers to his bulging crotch.

"I am ashamed," the pretty tour guide said, lowering her eyelashes. "I was so worried," Hana said. "At first, when the man said he was your friend and you had gone off with someone, I didn't think anything of it. After all, we were all having a wonderful time at Hanagahara."

"And you believed him just like that?" Jim asked incredulously. They had been trapped together in a bus locked in by snow ın the Japan Alps. The following morning the tour bus company had offered the passengers a free trip to a beautiful picnic spot, as a gesture of apology. Subsequently Jim and Andy had been drugged and spirited away from the party.

"He was so nice and he had paid for the entire picnic. He said he did not want foreigners going away with a bad impression of Japan . . ."

Andy laughed. "So that is how it was done. Slippery old Daddy Kitamura. Well, in the event, no harm was done. But how did you get here?"

"I had your address on the card you gave me. I got more and more worried, then finally took some leave and came to Tokyo. I came here several times but there was no one home. Eventually I found Teraoka-san . . ."

"I checked your apartment from time to time," Michiko joined in. Her blunt round face took on an officious expression and she crossed her blocky short legs self-consciously. "You said you would be away and we of course provide this service in the normal course of things. I noticed Someya-san coming by time and time again, and got, . . ." she laughed self-consciously, "a little bit suspicious. When she came to the police-box earlier I went along with her." Her wide mouth broadened into a smile. "I am glad it is a false alarm. Welcome back."

"Now that that's settled, how about some tea? Will you pour if I bring it, Michiko-san?" Andy winked.

The policewoman's freckles grew slightly more pronounced as her faced tinged with a blush. She had first gotten to know Andy over a cup of tea. He laughed aloud, leaned from his seat and kissed her lips. His hand slid up her skirt and met Jim's. She responded to the kiss for a second then pulled away, giggling.

"I am on duty Andy-san. I cannot stay, for I will be missed. . . ."

He started loosening his hold on her, then was struck by an idea. "You've been here for three minutes exactly. A total of five won't matter, will it?" he almost whispered. "Let me introduce you to an American custom called a quicky . . ."

"'Seven minutes," Jim said and rose to his feet. His dark eyes were on her figure.

Michiko's eyes darted past Andy's shoulder to Hana.

"No worry," he smiled into her eyes. "Hana and I have shared things in much the same way as we have shared with you. . . ."

Michiko nodded almost imperceptibly. Andy raised her to her feet. He pushed her against the armchair next to which she had been sitting and undid his watch, placing it on the low table beside them. He raised her blue-grey skirt with one hand and then pulled down her panty-hose and panties with the other. For brief second he dropped to his knees before her. His mouth was buried in the plentiful hairs at her crotch and his tongue hastily wet the delicate, scented lips. She leaned backwards and thrust her hips into his face. Hana was looking at her open-eyed, and Michiko realized it was with envy. The soft-hard tongue burned a fire of pleasure deep into her cunt and she spread her legs as far as she could, stretching the material of her underclothes while holding her skirt up.

Andy rose from her. His prick was jutting out of his pants. He bent slightly, presented it to the delicious moist lips and moved about for a few seconds until he could find her hole, then thrust home. She held onto his shoulders as he brutally pushed the length of his rampant prick up her still-dry channel. The pull of his hands on her hips, rough as it was, brought memories of shared pleasure and moistened her channel still further. They peered into one another's faces, both concerned not to mar her rather heavy makeup. The man's eyes glowed as his bottom oscillated, shuttling the length of his cock into her hungry channel. She cried out as his hairs mashed against her prominent soft pubis. Then her hands slid down and her blunt fingers dug hard into his rump. His frenzied motions almost raised her from the floor and he grunted with effort. Her knees gripped his thighs and she could feel the entire length of his cock as it ravaged her sensitive lips.

She thought her climax would never come, and all too soon she could feel the shuddering of Andy's frame as he drove himself to his own climax. The pressure of the spurts of his semen against the inner walls of her vagina caused the tiny beginning of an orgasmic shudder in her body. This was the first time she had paid attention to sensations other than her own lust, and for the first time she actually felt the hosing her insides were receiving from a man.

Michiko held tightly to Andy with her knees, knowing regretfully what was to follow. He bent his knees and his softening, glistening member withdrew from her. Again she could feel the tunneling of the man work through her own sensitized channel. Regretfully she was about to straighten up, when Jim stood before her, his cock erect and willing in his hand. Michiko sank back onto the chair back and opened herself further with her fingers. Her cunt lips were wet, drenched with the thick cream of Andy's cock. He was still standing to one side, looking at her and fingering his glistening penis. She blushed slightly, then looked down as Jim crouched and raised her into the air. Supported only by the upholstered chair back and Jim's hands, she assisted him by parting her slick lower lips. She watched as the broad purplish head of his cock nudged the soft entrance. Even as it widened the entrance she could feel the starting tremors of her own reaction mounting within her.

Jim's penetration was much easier. Drops of Andy's come had beaded her hairs and lubricated the channel so well that he slid up her with a speed she regretted slightly. But then he set to work, pumping his thighs hard into her, drawing his cock out to the tip, then pushing in again.

Hana, encouraged by Andy's wink and smile, walked around the fucking couple. She had never been able to examine things at such close range before. In the bus she had watched several couples out of the corner of her eyes, but had not had the nerve to examine them openly. In any case, it had been dark. Now she could indulge her curiosity to the full. .

She crouched beside the couple watching enviously as Jim's brown shaft, shining now with the shared juices in the policewoman's cunt, shuttled in and out. She could hardly believe that such a long pole could fit within the girls' belly, and yet knew from her own experience, that no discomfort was involved. As if she needed the proof, she could now see that Michiko's face was twisting into a rictus of pleasure. She examined the hairs between the two bodies, and then, feeling very daring, inserted a finger gingerly. The moss on the girl's belly was softer than the man's and both forests were damp, dappled with sticky, squishy wetness. She surprised herself by raising her fingers to her nose and sniffing the heavy musk that had adhered there. Then growing bolder, she held the shaft between two fingers. She felt the throbbing of the shaft and heard the cries of joy emitted by both man and woman. Then there was an intense thrumming in the shaft and her fingers were squeezed between the two heaving members. Hana's fingers were innundated by the excess fluid emitted by Jim's balls. trapped between the two heaving bodies, she felt the woman's slick tissues, the convolutions of cunt, with the back of her fingers just as she felt the softness of the man's balls, with just the tips of her fingers.

Jim rose from Michiko, still smiling. The quivers of her insides were just subsiding. he was pleased and unsurprised to find the pretty tour-guide's hand resting on the base of his cock and fingering the top of his ball-bag. Michiko opened her eyes slowly, recovering from her orgasm, and rose from the padded chairback.

''Wonderful things, armchairs,'' Jim whispered. She smiled in agreement.

Andy was ready with a moist hand towel. He applied it thoroughly while smiling up into her eyes. Then he pulled her underclothes up to her thighs. She finished the job, though her fingers were unsteady because of the dying fluttering in her groin. Her skirt was smoothed into place. She looked at the three faces and smiled shyly. Andy held the watch up for her inspection.

''Five minutes exactly,'' he said. They all laughed and then walked her to the door.

''Come back as soon as you are off shift.'' Jim said. ''All three of us will be waiting. Michiko bowed formally and walked out as the two brothers turned to Hana.

''Second act coming up,'' Andy said as they bore her giggling form to a bedroom. Then he added in Japanese accented English. ''Not quicky. Srowry now.''

CHAPTER 2

THE MISSIONARY POSITION

The day was gloomy and rather grim. Kaoru peered out the window blearily. It was his day off and he found that he did not have the energy to go anywhere. The hangover from the previous night's drinking did not help. He staggered into the tiny kitchen of his apartment and drank some water. The buzzing in his head grew. He shook himself irritably, then realized it was the phone. Hunting under the rumpled bedclothes he discovered the instrument. For a moment he was tempted to ignore it, then thought it might be the company, and his loyalty to the firm took over.

"Yanagisato-san?" It was a female voice. Slightly foreign.

"Huh?" he said. He knew no forei. . . . Just a minute, memory flowered in his mind. The woman from America . . . Her name almost unpronounceable. . . .

"Yanagisato-san? This is Millicent. . . ."

"Purdue-san!" he suddenly remembered.

She laughed into the receiver at the other side. "Yes. I was afraid you had forgotten me. . . ."

His loins grew warm and he was conscious his cock was starting to unfurl. "I am sorry," he said. "I am a little bit disoriented. This is my day off and I have barely woken up. . . .''

''Wonderful!'' she said in the abrupt manner that he had come to associate with foreigners. As a tour-bus driver he had met many in the previous two years. ''Could I come and see you?'' There was some tension in her voice, and he wondered what its source was. He looked around at his little rented apartment. Well, it could be nicer but. . . .

''Where are you Miricento-san?'' he asked.

''Just around the corner from the address you gave me . . .''

''Come right away,'' he said and let the phone down softly. For a moment he stood there in his underwear. The memory of the blonde curls on her thighs and lower belly mesmerized him and his cock throbbed again. Then the reality of his room burst into his consciousness and he erupted into a frenzy of action.

She rang the buzzer and he opened the door. She stepped into the small shoe space and looked around her. It had taken her much courage to make up her mind to travel to Nagoya just to see the young man she had met once, and she thought for the last time, in a bus in the Kiso mountains. But the memory of the night they had spent in one another's arms, trapped in a snowbound bus had haunted her for weeks until she had decided to track him down. Taking leave from the mission had been difficult but not impossible, and here she was. She knew it was brazen and immoral: he was not only a strange man, he was a heathen as well. But he was her first real sexual pleasure, and masturbation, though fun, always led her back to thinking of his broad-shouldered smooth-skinned figure. She looked past him as she undid her shoes to distract herself from the smell and sight of him. The tiny apartment was in perfect order. New *tatami* mats gleamed and there was even a small scroll hanging from one of the wall beams. She bowed to distract herself from his nearness and he did the same. They straightened at the same time and he saw her eyes fix on his crotch where the rod of his masculinity struggled against the fabric of his slacks. She raised her face to his. Her mouth was open and lips moist. She reached behind her and clicked the doorknob button to locked, then swayed forward.

Kaoru reached for her, fearing she was about to fall and his hand brushed against her full breasts. Her hands caught at his hips and they were suddenly falling back. He clutched at air and came up with two handfulls of soft mounds that squirmed against his palms even as he sought to cushion their fall onto the hard linoleum. They hit with a thump and Kaoru was conscious of Millicent's untrained fingers fumbling at his fly. She gave a triumphant cry as his cock burst forth. Her mouth clamped to his as he tore at her blouse, exposing the full fabric-covered breasts. He clawed at the cloth and pulled the cups down. Her full breasts bounced back in his hands, just as he felt her rise then impale herself onto his erect cock.

Millicent squealed with delight as she felt the meaty length of his rod penetrate her tight insides. She thought she could feel every inch of his erection rub against her sensitive interior tissues. Her blonde hair fell about her face as she shook her uncontrollably with pleasure. His hands squeezed passionately at her jugs, pulling them painfully downwards towards his cruel waiting mouth. She surrendered herself, falling forward, supported only by his grasping hands as he led first one and then another pale pink nipple to his lips and teeth.

She shrugged hurriedly out of here torn blouse, then pulled frenziedly at his shirt. She wanted to feel his smooth skin against hers. The shirt resisted and she tore at it in a frenzy of lust as powerful as the touch of his teeth on the skin of her tits. Then his body was free and she rubbed herself over his chest as far as she could reach. Kaoru released her full mounds and surrendered to the sensation of her hands, breasts and belly against his torso. He raised his hips slightly and slid his pants fully off him, finally kicking them off with drumming heels.

As Millicent slithered and rubbed herself against his

chest, he set to work to explore her body. This was the first time he had ever been mounted by a woman and he was determined to exploit the novelty. His hands traced her legs sliding up along her calves on either side of his thighs, then over her knees. Then he approached her full bum, sliding his hands along the silky surface. She moaned heavily into his shoulder, her lips leaving a slick wetness he enjoyed. His hands parted her buns and he toyed with the plentiful hair that lined the crack. He explored her ass hole with one finger, shyly almost, afraid to startle her. It too was overlaid to his delight with tight tiny curls. She was starting to move up and down his slick pole as his exploring fingers traced the length of his own shaft to the juncture with her flesh. Her inner lips were distended around the pole and he pinched the tissue roughly between his fingers and the tumescent shaft.

Soon the pleasure of the moments was overtaking both of them. Her mouth clamped to his lips and her tongue searched out his in the warmth of his oral cavity. It was like fucking a man, Millicent thought, penetrating him roughly with her tongue just as he was penetrating her roughly with his cock. Then his strong hands grasped her hips and his blunt fingers dug deeply into the soft flesh that padded her hipbones.

She squealed aloud into his mouth as the first violent waves of her climax rose to engulf her. Her fingers dug into her own breasts and into the muscles of his chest indifferently. She wished he were deeper into her, and she forced herself onto the hardness of his cock, trying to swallow the entire length just as she was forcing her tongue into his mouth.

As if reading her mind Kaoru raised his hips as high as she could, until the entire weight of her body was suspended on the bridge of his body. When that was not enough he gave a great cry and pushed violently to one side. She spread her legs as they rolled over and he hammered himself deeply into her waiting cunt, spiking her like a spread butterfly onto the linoleum of his kitchen.

The cold of the linoleum against their naked bodies and the sound of their panting brought them back to their senses. Kaoru turned his head and smiled weakly at her. ''I had the *futon* all prepared,'' he said. She smiled back, accepting the statement as an apology. Instead of answering she stroked his cheek lightly. ''We will still use it.'' she said firmly.

''Would you like something to drink?''

''I will serve,'' Millicent said, determined to try and play the proper Japanese woman. ''And after, we'll do this,'' with great daring she rose to one elbow, leaned over his form and sucked lightly at the softening tip of his cock. ''And this,'' she led his hand between her legs and deliberately slipped one of his fingers into her overflowing cunt. ''And lots of other things.''

Kaoru rose, his half-erect cock before him like a limp standard and headed for the spread *futon* while Millicent watched his firm ass and sucked her teeth thoughtfully. There was so much to be done.

CHAPTER 3

AND THE WORD IS FLESH

"You remember me, don't you?"

Andy peered at the blonde, smiled, then had to admit he didn't.

"We were on a bus, several months ago . . ." She had the grace to blush a bit as Andy grinned. The missionary girl, of course.

"Come on in," he said. "What can we do for you?"

She sat, sipping at the coffee he had offered her, saying nothing but absorbing the small apartment with her eyes. "I, . . . I'm sorry to intrude this way, but I don't know anyone in Tokyo. . . . I know we are barely acquainted but. . . ."

Jim looked at Andy out of the corner of his eyes. They had come once or twice before to the aid of damsels in distress. It had proven to be fun, but they weren't really in the business, and this prim-looking and drably-dressed female did not at all look like the kind who would enjoy their company. Or they hers.

"I'm in a terrible mess," she laughed artificially. "And I would like your advice."

"Sure," Andy said automatically.

"You see, for the past three weeks I've been living with this Japanese man. The driver from the bus in fact . . ."

"Well, I see that bus was the start of several long and fruitful friendships," Jim said. He licked the corners of his mouth suggestively. Millicent found it hard not to blush. She knew he had seen Kaoru pumping away between her legs. "Then what's the problem?"

This time she did blush, then dithered, trying to avoid a *too* detailed explanation. There were two problems really. First, Kaoru, loving as he was, was still Japanese. He expected her to behave, particularly in public, as a Japanese woman should. And though she had been taught to be meek, the minimal demands of her mission training had not prepared her for the public meekness of the Japanese woman, and she had no knowledge whatsoever of the machinery of indirect control Japanese women used on their menfolk. Secondly, she had the feeling that satisfying and delightful as sex with Kaoru was, there was still something missing. She did not know if he felt the same way, but some of the passion in their lovemaking had become mechanical. he was, after all, as emotionally insulated as she, and neither of them knew how to express their sexual preferences and demands fully. As far as Millicent was concerned, she was not even able to articulate those demands and preferences to herself, let alone to her man. She temporized with the two young men. "I'm sort of in a dilemma. I need some sort of job, and I need to think about . . . about my relationship to Kaoru. He's a heathen, you know?"

Jim shrugged. He himself was one as well, so what?

"Aren't you a missionary of some sort?" Andy asked curiously. "Surely they take care of their people?"

"Yes. Actually, that is, no. I, ah, took some unofficial leave from my post and didn't return . . ." She hung her head shamefacedly.

"And what are you going to do now?" Jim asked sympathetically.

"I don't know. Teach English I guess. Or whatever."

"You want to stay the night here? We'll do whatever is necessary to save you from their evil clutches. Skulk around alleys, uncover the evil in its lair.'' They went of into one of their Shadow routines, and Millicent looked at them in open-mouthed alarm.

"Its all right. We're just a little bit crazy." Andy consoled her; patting the skirt over her knees.

"At least I am. He's a *lot* crazy, Jim, seconded, patting the other leg.

She leaned back onto the couch, unconsciously smoothing the woolen skirt over her thighs. She was conscious of the four eyes following her movements. For a moment she felt a sense of alarm, then a picture of Kaoru came into her mind and she stroked her thighs deliberately. They had quarrelled and she had left him in a huff, his beautiful eyes still staring at her angrily. Well, this would serve him right. In any case, she had little to hide from these two young men, they had seen here body on the bus. And they were both so attractive too.

"If there's any little thing I can do here for you?" she asked in what she hoped was a sexy voice. She raised both hands to her hair and piled the yellow mass high, exposing the shape of her breasts against the stretched fabric of her drab blouse.

"Why, there are a couple of things, Jim said, breathing warmly into her ear. His hand slid up her waist and squeezed the prominent nipple that had hardened under her prim bra. On her other side Andy had knelt and his hands were gliding delightfully up the length of her stocking. For a moment she wondered if this were the right thing. She was betraying her training, and her love for Kaoru, but then the sensory pleasure of two pairs of male hands on her body overrode everything else and she surrendered to her own pleasure.

"Can we get to a bed?" she whispered.

Obligingly they led her to Andy's room. She pulled down the covers, and turned, unsurprised to find both men naked. They had similar body shapes, and besides a slight difference in coloring, looked identical, even to the size and shapes of their pricks. Her palms sweaty with excitement she undressed, dropping her calf-length skirt on the floor, her white blouse and brassiere following. They looked at her and licked their lips and she backed onto the bed, falling there with her legs open.

"God, what a fuzz," Andy whispered to himself. Millicent heard the words but they did not register. She had never seen another naked woman, and had no idea how they were constructed, so her own golden-hirsute belly and thighs were unsurprising to her. As if drawn by a magnet, Andy crouched between her legs. His tongue flicked out and attacked her waiting clitoris with relish. Sucking and nibbling he burrowed his way into the mossy grotto, pulling and nipping at the hairs. Jim, more controlled, lay down beside her and ran his hands over her body. He stroked her waist and then tugged at her breasts. She pulled his head to her body and he obligingly sucked first one, then the other of her breasts. Her blood ran warm and she could feel the exquisite penetration by Andy's tongue. She closed her eyes.

A male figure mounted her without preamble. She felt fingers between her legs and the knob was brushed against the plentiful hair of her pussy, making its way through the damp thicket until it pressed against the split between her legs. Slowly the knob widened its entrance, and as she closed her eyes she could feel the length of the shaft make its way up her moist and demanding channel. Then she felt the pressure of his balls bag against her distended buttocks. For a second the man lay in her, supporting his upper torso with his forearms. She wondered which one it was, but did not want to spoil the poignancy of feeling in her sex. A mouth nibbled slowly at her upper arm and she shivered, knowing it was the other twin. Then the one inside her started moving. Faster and faster his cock pistoned in and out of her willing receptacle. She raised her knees to aid them, and then a pair of hand pulled her ankles over the heaving buttocks. She smiled and grunted in joy and gratitude and a mouth descended on her own. Hungrily she sucked in the male tongue, battling it with her own. Hands were on her breasts now, squeezing them painfully, then relenting. . Strumming her erect nipples, then squeezing them strongly. Her eyes closed she rode to a climax and was conscious of the moisture slipping out of her and running between her buns to stain the sheet. A massive heaving and wriggling of the cock in her told her that her lover was about to come. She concentrated on the sensation and was rewarded by feeling her insides being hosed by his powerful contractions. For a second or two he lay on her, stretched fully out. She bore the weight happily.

As she was about to open her eyes the man slipped off her relaxed, yet still demanding body. The other took his place. This time his cock found her gluey, moisture-filled cunt without any hesitation. The long male shaft hurled up the length of her channel and she gasped in delight. She rubbed the length of his muscular calves with the soles of her feet and clutched at his sweating back. The other one started feeling her breasts. This time a bit more forcefully then before. She raised her knees as high as she could and was rewarded by being able to feel the full weight of his pubis ramming his cock fiercely into her. Their mouths roved over her body, sucking and licking just as their hands seemed to be everywhere, inadvertently even stroking and poking at the areas she did not associate with sex. She climaxed in a sustained ongoing rush, her insides contracting powerfully around the male organ. The man flooded her full slick insides with his sperm, grinding-his hips mercilessly into her yielding calyx of flesh. Then he slipped out of her, and to her delight, was replaced again by his twin.

The room was in complete darkness by the time the three of them stopped moving. The sheet under her hips was soaked with their joined emissions. She felt the thatch of hair that grew on her belly and thighs cautiously. The perky golden curls were mashed down, floating in a sea of moisture, plastered in sea-weed tangles to her skin. She sniffed surreptitiously at the warm earthy odor that rose into the air. Someone's belly rumbled in the darkness and someone else laughed.

"We should really kneel down and thank the Lord for our pleasure," she said, idly stroking the heads resting on her tits. The two men ignored her, and their regular breathing seemed to indicate they were well on their way to sleep.

Millicent spent the following day trying to line up a job. Most of the job offers were for low-pay English teaching. Two were for waitress jobs, but one of those, the offer was so horrendous she barely dared even think about it. But it paid well, very well indeed, a small voice whispered wickedly into her ear. Jim and Andy took her out to eat *oden* stew. The idea of eating at one of the small stalls where working class Japanese congregated to eat boiled fish paste, seaweed, eggs and vegetables had never entered her mind. The taste she found was not fishy at all, pleasant in fact, though she rebelled against the rubbery sweet boiled squid that they pressed on her. Strolling back to the apartment, she returned to her original tack again, trying to get the two men to admit the need for their salvation. The missionary fervor in her was still strong. She had left Kaoru partly for the same reason. He was perfectly willing to enjoy her, and delighted in her company, but he was also totally uninterested in what she had to say. And though she had daringly slept with both Andy and Jim, she knew they would not even imagine the sorts of things Kaoru had imagined, and suggested, doing with her. The very thought of his desires, expressed in veiled terms though they were, made her blush. She loved him deeply, but even to the man of her dreams she would not permit the liberties he had wanted to assume. And besides, the practical side of her said, she could not live on his meagre salary forever. Once established, she could perhaps call on him again. . . .

They entered the apartment and Andy stretched hugely. "Time for bed." he looked at her suggestively. "Don't you have any other clothes than these? You'd look great in a mini . . ."

"Or in nothing at all," Jim leered and reached for her.

"Not before we thank the Lord for our benefits," she said evading the reaching hand. Bringing these two young men to the right path would serve as penance for her earlier thoughts about the forbidden job.

"What the hell are you talking about Millie?" Andy said. "In the first place, neither of us is a Christian, in the second, we can't stand being preached to . . ."

"And in the third place, I'm dying for a fuck." Jim added.

"I'd love to, Jim dear. But I cannot without recognizing the bounty . . ."

"Loosen up Millicent," Andy said. "Hey, we're all enjoying ourselves, right?"

"Will you shut up you sanctimonious bitch?" Jim asked angrily. He had less patience than Andy for most nonsense, particularly the sort that kept him from sex. "What the hell do you mean spouting this stuff in our house?"

"I have to. It's my calling," she said somewhat heatedly.

"You were thrown out of your order because you were making it with a Japanese man," Jim retorted heatedly. "Now shut up. More importantly, lets fuck." he reached for her again and the lust rose in her groin at the feeling of his hands on her. She pushed him away and stepped into Andy's arms. "You'll agree, wont you Andy?"

"Of course I won't," he chuckled. He pulled her to the ground with him, pulled her head around and stuck his tongue between her lips. She pushed against him hard, but by then Jim was upon her.

She made no attempt to resist beyond an initial kick as they pulled her legs apart. She had worn no underclothes when they had left to eat. Her golden fuzz obscured the wicked wink of her pink cunt lips. Jim dove for her snatch, his mouth clamping to the juicy folds while Andy leaped for her torso and began sucking her tits.

"If this is that only way to lead you to salvation, then so be it," she whispered in resignation as she stroked his head.

They mounted her brutally and without thought to her pleasure. The hard driving cocks stimulated her quickly to a writhing orgasm of her own. She felt fingers tracing patterns on her skin, actually feeling her privates as they fucked, and for the first time it occurred to her that the fingers on the entrance to her rear hole were not there accidentally. To divert attention from that area, she pulled at Jim's hips, leading him to her mouth. He posed over her for a moment, directing his semi-hard cock at her face. She saw the glistening red shaft descend, then sucked at it greedily. The shaft hardened in her mouth as he began cautiously pumping into her. Andy watched them, then adjusted his strokes to those of his brother. Together they shafted her in unison, and once again Millicent felt the tide of passion rise in her body. For a single moment she cried out "Kaoru!": but the cry was muffled by the meaty cock plunging into her mouth. her own orgasm was dwindling when she felt Jim stiffen for a long moment. A dribble of viscous fluid spurted out of the tip of his cock, and she knew that he was coming into her mouth. For a moment she felt like gagging, then managed to convince herself that the taste was not much different from the *oden* she had eaten. Then she tasted the fluid hungrily, realizing that it merely enhanced the taste she had had in her mouth since his insertion: the taste of her own vaginal juices. She closed her eyes again, surrendering completely to the power of his passion.

"I have to leave," she said sadly the following morning. "You will understand. I cannot live with you, since you are sinners. But I will find a place today, and start my own work. And come and visit you often."

"For the god of our souls?" Jim cracked. The early morning tea had rekindled his spirits.

"Yes. Of course. And for the pleasure of your bodies."

''That's one crazy lady,'' Jim said over his coffee cup as he gazed at the closing door.

''Good riddance,'' Andy shrugged. ''She might have been quite a lay with some education by Professor Middler and his assistant though.''

''Professor Suzuki and *his* assistant, you mean.''

''Whatever. Now in the matter of a new house . . .'' The argument about moving to larger quarters had been going on for several weeks. They were in no hurry and enjoyed the leisurely wrangling.

CHAPTER 4

NOT CASSIUS, NO, NOT EVEN LIKE

His head still full of figures, Jim stumped to the door. On the threshold stood a plump, almost fat, Japanese girl. She had long smooth hair that fell past her shoulders, almost to her waist. She was dressed in a severe suit. A large cloisonne brooch held her white blouse closed. She had the air of a saleswoman expecting to make a deal. A tough one. Her face, which bore the marks of a recent case of acne, looked familiar.

"Suzuki-san? You remember me? I told you you must. Is Midlaa-san in?"

Recognition swam back into memory. There had been nine of them. Nine members of a university climbing club on their final trip before graduation. He and Andy had been searching for the headquarters of their fathers' company in a desultory sort of way, and had spent the night with the nine virgins in a mountain inn. Or at least, they had been virgins when they had gone to bed. And one of them had said, . . . had said ". . . this has been super. My name is Baba Matsuko. Remember it. I will remember you. Both of you."

"Baba Matsuko-san," he bowed gravely.

"Ah then, you do remember me. I am pleased." She looked at him commandingly and raised an eyebrow.

"Please come in," he said and moved back. "Andy is out."

She walked regally into the apartment. There was something almost intimidating about her. She projected physical and personal power. Without saying a word she first examined the room gravely, then sat down on an overstuffed armchair.

"What could I do for you?" Jim asked. The break from work was welcome, and he wondered whether. . . .

"I will wait," she said politely. "When Andy-san returns . . ."

"Tea then?" he asked.

She accepted the cup, smiling perforce at his male clumsiness in pouring it, and nibbled at a small cake he offered. "I can never resist sweetmeats," she said reflectively. A rueful smile curved her mouth.

"How did you find us?" Jim asked to make conversation.

She looked surprised "It was easy. There are not many Middlers in the English phone book, and in any case I remembered you mentioning your university. I asked and was told your address. Here is Andy-san now."

Andy was slower to recognize her than Jim had been. She was the first one he had mounted on that memorable night, but the light had been dim, and there were others, prettier ones, that followed her.

She sat bolt upright on the armchair examining them as both young men examined her in return. For a second it seemed as if she had lost some of her confidence, but then her spine straightened some more and she stopped playing with a strand of hair that had fallen over her face.

"I have tried many men since that night. Casually usually. I am not a beautiful woman, but before I grow fat, or have a family, I want to learn and to enjoy. You were the first, and the best teachers I have had. I see you have no woman here . . ."

Fearing what was coming, not intending to be forced into any sort of relationship, Andy opened his mouth to speak. She forestalled him by patting the air in front of her and bobbing a bow. He desisted.

"I will be here for only a short time, time enough for you to enjoy me, and for me to learn. If you wish, I will help you with house and domestic things."

"How much is a short time?" Jim asked, a tone of sourness in his words. He was being manipulated into something he could not see all the consequences of. "We are in the process of moving to a new place, you see."

"Only a few days. Once I found you I took a few days off my work. I am a clerk in a large company, but they will not let me off too long. Three-four days at most. I will help you move." The last was said with a forceful determination which both men knew they would be unable to override.

"Won't your company object?" Andy asked curiously.

A smile which transformed her face appeared briefly on her lips. "My father is the company president."

They laughed with her.

They rose together, not sure how to start. She turned and led them unerringly into the first bedroom. Andy's large bed dominated the small Japanese room. She stood in the middle of the empty space, her toes in their white stockings curling into the rich carpet. The two men looked at her almost shyly. She slipped off the jacket of her red suit, folding it and hanging it neatly on a chair. She looked at herself in the mirror. Her plumpness showed and she stroked the side of her stomach reflectively, then ran the zipper of her skirt down, stepped out of the garment, and folded it too.

The two men took a step towards her. She eyed them with surprise, started to say something, then subsided when she felt their hands upon her. They stripped her together. The unpinned brooch was laid carefully aside, and her white blouse quickly followed. She had wide shoulders and powerful looking arms, in concert with the rest of her: full, not yet run to fat, powerful looking. For a moment the look of wistful shyness came into her face again. She looked far more vulnerable and much less determined than she had looked before. Then her character reasserted itself and her features firmed again.

Noting the changes, Jim kissed her neck and then her shoulders while Andy knelt to divest her of her stockings and panties. He kissed his way up her solid leg, taking special care with the soft insides of her thighs and the full brush that sprouted from the bottom of her belly. Jim kissed her mouth than turned his attention to her wide breasts with their flat aureolae and nipples. She stroked their head softly and yet, somehow, conveyed a sense of command in all she did. They rose to stand on either side of her, then turned her about to face the large mirror Andy had installed for occasions such as the current one. She looked thoughtfully at the trio in the mirror. The woman she saw was short, and nothing could hide the bulk of her build. She had a nice smile, which transformed her broad, rather coarse features. Her breasts were solid and erect, flat on her chest rather than prominent. Her belly was smooth, her hips wide and well padded. Her legs were the archetypical *daikon ashi*, so prized in peasant women, so despised by modern girls in mini-skirts which she could never attempt to wear: thick and muscular. She was conscious of the two hands that were both in the crack of her ass and examined her consorts. Their slim bodies and postures were so alike she could find no difference between them, except perhaps for some slighter more hairiness on the *gaijin* looking one. Their penises were still barely erect, a state she liked to examine penises in. They sprouted, promising action, from their nests of hair. They examined her as frankly as she did them, smiling slightly.

"I want you to do everything a woman and two men can do together," she said. "In due time I will marry, and I want my enjoyment before then. I also want to be able to please my husband properly."

"Sit side by side, here, on the bed," she ordered.

The two men obeyed and she knelt before them. Both cocks rose in her grasp and she began a lollipop, licking one shaft then the other. Her broad tongue eliciting sparks of pleasure from the shafts. Both men bent forward and stroked her broad ass. Their other hands were busy with her hanging breasts. Her breathing quickened as she tried to imagine what to do with them first. She wanted them inside, her, those beautiful cocks would have to please her properly first, before any fancy stuff. Her mouth, of course, then even the other entrance, perhaps both of them, one in the front hole, the other in the rear, if that was at all possible. She wished she had larger breasts: it would be nice to have a prick rubbing there, the juices squirting over her chest. She wondered what their cream tasted like. One of her recent lovers had ejaculated prematurely, fountaining over her belly. He had been extremely embarrassed by the incident but she had found it interesting, touching the stuff and smearing it over her belly and her pussy hairs. Yes, definitely they would do all that. But later, later. Just now she needed them in her. Both of them. Which one first? She watched the cocks grow in her hands and then bent to suck one of them in. This too she had learned recently, and even been complimented on her performance by the man she had chosen. Her free hand surreptitiously examined her wet channel. She shoved her fingers in gradually as the men stroked her broad back and squeezed her tits with growing urgency. All five fingers fitted in, and when she pushed them apart, she felt no pain. Th idea that had been hidden before blazed to overt certainty.

Matsuko stopped sucking at Jim's shaft and stroked it softly with her fist. It took but a minute to make up her mind. She could see the almost uncontrollable lust in both men's eyes. Rising quickly she squatted over Andy's lap. Jim looked on patiently with some disappointment. Then the pleasure of the maleness in her snatch overcame all else and Matsuko settled her not inconsiderable weight onto the spike that drove for her vitals, sending off electric surges as it made its way into her.

She looked into Andy's still face, then pushed him

backwards. His feet were still on the floor as she rested her hands on his firm chest, massaging the muscles. She hoped neither of the men would object to what she had in mind, hoped too that they were sophisticated and experienced enough to appreciate it. She crouched low on Andy's body, then motioned Jim to stand up.

"You too," she whispered.

He spread her full fat buns, exposing the clenched dot that was her anus, touching it experimentally with her finger. Beneath it the forest of black hairs was distended by Andy's pale shaft lying motionless but readily in her channel.

"No, not there," she said clearly. "That is for later. Put it in together with Andy-san." She peered at him encouragingly over her shoulder.

Jim looked at her doubtfully. For a fairly recent virgin she seemed awfully adventurous, and he had no desire to injure her.

"I can take it," she whispered. "I want it. I need both of you. Now!" The last word was an undeniable command. Jim moved up behind her, aiming his cock at her stuffed entrance. She bent forward and he pushed in, feeling reluctant muscles part before his thrust.

"Not there!" She muttered and pulled away. Even the pain was delightful, she thought as she redirected his efforts towards the right hole. "Don't pay any attention," she instructed him. "Push! Hard!" Andy reached for her breasts and she closed her eyes, concentrating on the tactile sensations.

Jim pushed forward, still cautiously. The entrance yielded reluctantly. He could see sweat break out on Matsuko's broad brow. Still she gritted her teeth and pulled him in, guiding Jim's shaft along Andy's and into her burning flesh with a determined fist.

She felt the head of the cock slip finally into her hole. The pain was exquisite. A burning tearing sensation, not unlike, but much more intense than her first fuck pervaded her body. She cried out incoherently, giving vent to her pain and to her triumph, as the monster double-prick made its way safely up her soft flesh. She was conscious of Jim's hands on her broad ass, and of the distension of her tissues. Then overriding the pain, she started forcing herself backwards onto the punishing male members. At first her body resisted, wanting only to flee the tearing sensation. But soon, as her juices began to flow and as her vagina accustomed itself to the double penetration, pleasure began to supersede the pain. Soon she was moving freely, stroking the bodies beneath and above her, her mouth reaching for what it could and being rewarded with kisses and fondlings for her effort.

She started grunting, high pitched delirious sounds, as her body rose to the occasion and an orgasm, the most powerful she had ever felt, rose in the depths of her loins. "Together! I want us to come together!" She wailed as the waves of dizzying sensation threatened to overcome her. The two men responded with inarticulate cries, their cocks pounding at her flesh in unison, trapped by her muscular power and the commanding presence of her personality.

The relief when she crested was overwhelming. She clawed at Andy's chest leaving bright stripes and turned her head to bite violently at Jim's shoulder. Both men responded to her violent throes with jerkings and heavings of their own. The burning sensation in her cunt, still distended painfully, was finally extinguished by the hosings from their twinned pricks. White male essence flooded her interior and assisted the final movements of the three lovers.

They subsided slowly and pulled away from her. For a time she lay there, her eyes open but still looking back at their concerned faces. Her body was drenched with sweat, and the memory of the burning and tearing in her vagina was still there, though the sensation itself was gone with the flood.

She rolled over to her back, spreading her legs. "See? No harm has been done." The two men relaxed and she turned to the mirrors. Lying on her side she raised on leg in the air and examined the reflection of her overflowing vagina. The inner lips were still bright, angry red, but the hole seemed little larger than its original size. She squeezed her interior muscles and a wave of white sperm welled out and ran over her inner thigh. "I am very strong, you see. Both inside and out," she said complacently.

Silently they laid themselves down on either side of her and helped her explore her body anew. She looked at the large *shunga* print hanging on the wall. It had taken all the profits of one of Andy's deals, but he thought it worthwhile. It was unsigned, perhaps from the school of Hokusai. It depicted two women, newly risen from the bath, exploring one another hungrily.

"Have you ever made love to a woman?" Andy asked her curiously.

She shook her head. "I wanted to try it too. There is a young woman in my father's company, where I work. But she did not get my hints, or perhaps I did not know how to go about it."

"And in the climbing club?"

"We played together in the tub, but you see, there were so many others more beautiful than myself . . ."

"We will arrange it," Jim said, his eyes glowing. "Yes, definitely. We will find someone appropriate."

CHAPTER 5

SOMETHING BORROWED . . .

''Andy-san?'' the whining baby-doll voice was familiar. Muzzy with figures from a spreadsheet on a late afternoon, Andy's cock still rose to the challenge.

''Yes Natsumi. How are you?''

''I am well Andy-san. I have not heard from you for so long . . .'' There was a world of suggestion in her voice, but with Natsumi nothing was simple. Besides, Andy took some pleasure in tormenting her. As much, in fact, as she enjoyed tormenting him.

''So?'' he asked.

There was a confused silence at the other end of the line, then the secretary's voice said ''Can I see you?''

Rejoicing in his petty victory Andy said ''Now!''

''No, I cannot come. I am still at work. At six? Will you take me to a bar?''

He grinned at the mouthpiece. ''Sure, why not. Just so long as I can poke your lovely little hole later.''

Her silence continued for a second and then she decided to laugh uncertainly. ''I want to see you,'' she breathed into his ear.

The bar she led him to was not the sort of place he would have gone into alone. Rather than a serious drinking place such as Sato's which he and Jim frequented in their neighborhood, this place was concerned with atmosphere. People seemed to come there more to be seen than for anything else. The furniture was painted pink and canary yellow. Art-deco posters, a style Andy detested, were hung on the walls. There was a smattering of people at some of the tables, and the bar itself was to small to accommodate any more than four patrons at a time. The bar sold multicolored cocktails: an innovation that Japanese had not taken to fully, Andy was pleased to note.

They sat at the table and Andy examined Natsumi with pleasure and at length. He had never understood the hold she had on him. She was rather small and slim, except for quite full buttocks. Her dark brown hair brown hair was curled as usual. When she spoke English, which she did often, she spoke it in a whining sort of singsong which Andy thought to be artificial. Perhaps her greatest charm was the conscious and constant cock-teasing she engaged in, rejecting verbally and encouraging physically anything he wanted to do to her. He licked his lips, trying to provoke a reaction, but she watched his contortions with placid eyes, as if totally unaware of the thoughts beneath his face.

Perturbed again by her seeming indifference, he put one hand beneath the table and slid it up the length of her nylon covered thigh. She permitted his hand under her skirt for a brief second, then clamped her thighs together.

"Andy-san!" she whined in protest.

He grinned back, confident of the roles they were both playing.

"I want to fuck you," he said brutally. "Let's get out of her so you can suck my cock." His hand tightened on the soft flesh of her thigh. She was wearing stockings and garters he noted: a present he had given her some months before. He squeezed the soft bare flesh, wondering if any of the other patrons were watching the show.

"No! You must not do this Andy-san," she said sternly. "You must behave properly!" The tiny tip of her tongue flicked out for a second and she squirmed uncomfortably in her seat, then bent and sipped at the horrible green cocktail she had ordered.

"You say you will do anything for me, yet you always whine about it," Andy complained.

"But Andy-san," she said. "I am your steady but you don't see me very often. I know you see other girls . . ."

"You want us to continue?" he asked roughly.

She nodded. "Yes, Andy-san. You know I am yours. . . . I don't mind the other girls. But you said I am your steady date." The baby-doll whine, like a wheedling five year old was back in her voice. The tone irritated him, and yet when they were together, fucking, it drove him to heights of aggressive performance. He looked at her speculatively, wondering how far he could push her. What the hell, there were plenty more fish in the sea if she decided to leave. . . .

"You see that girl over there? The one sitting alone, long hair?"

Natsumi nodded, then turned back to him expectantly.

"Go over to her and tell her your boyfriend wants to make love to her. Be polite to her. Seduce her. I want you to get her to come with me."

"You are really my boyfriend, Andy-san? I am glad. I do not mind if you have other girls," She looked at him wide eyed, then added thoughtfully "No."

"Natsumi . . ." he growled at her

"Telling her you want to make love to her is too direct. Not Japanese. I will think of something. You sit here." She rose and slipped from the table, then walked over to the other girl.

He smiled down at his beer then took another sip. This might be interesting. He had never had a girl pander for him before. Success or failure would not matter. Either way he would have fun. He looked up. Natsumi was sitting with the girl, engaged in conversation. The girl with the long hair was rather thin. He had chosen her because she had been sitting by herself for some time, staring emptily into space. She looked in his direction and he smiled faintly at her. Finally the two women rose and approached him. he stood up as well.

"This is Ohashi Atsuko. Andy Midlaa-san."

"*Hajimemashite*," he said politely, bowing. She regarded him for one moment out of dark expressionless eyes.

"Atsuko-san is an artist," Natsumi said chattily. She pointed to the large portfolio the girl carried.

"That's very nice. What sort of stuff do you do?" Andy asked, barely masking his impatience.

Atsuko opened the portfolio. The paintings inside were flaring swirls of color. Dark red, purples, blues and greens clashed and fought with black backgrounds. The colors gave a gloomy and foreboding image to the choices of subject. Human figures, both male and female were depicted in varying poses. Both the nudes and the dressed studies were gruesome. Most of the pictures depicted spouting fountains of blood, bodies cut open with their limbs and organs exposed, their skin blistered with unseen weapons.

"Very nice," Andy said politely though his stomach turned at the choice of subject. "She draws very well." This last was true. The artist had captured the physiological details with painful, almost neurotic attention to detail.

"I work for a comic book publisher," Atsuko said.

That explained many things, Andy thought. Japanese comic books, read by adults and not just children, specialized often in scenes of gratuitous violence. It was as if some hidden corner of Japanese culture exposed itself through a mask of drawings.

"Shall we go?" he smiled cheerily. This might turn out to be *extremely* interesting. He wondered if Jim was home already. He knew that Jim often enjoyed violent sex, and this girl seemed to be a prime candidate . . .

The apartment was empty. Atsuko followed Natsumi and Andy into his bedroom without any protest or indication of her feelings. He wondered what Natsumi had said to her. He and Natsumi had chatted animatedly on the way home from Shinjuku. In the taxi he had sat between the two girls, his arms around both. He had fondled Natsumi freely, and she had, in contrast to her usual protestations, giggled freely and allowed him full access to her self. Atsuko had tolerated his hand on her breast, but had then captured him and kept it there, restraining any further explorations.

They entered Andy's bedroom and he turned to Atsuko and raised a hand to her small bosom. She stood quit still, barely breathing as he fondled her. His other hand slipped from her slim waist to her crotch. She pushed him away, unspeaking, and moved to the side, her eyes wide. Andy grinned and shrugged.

"Take off your blouse," he ordered Natsumi, his head cocked to one side. She unbuttoned her white blouse obediently, her eyes darting from Andy to Atsuko and back. Without further instructions she pulled off the straps of her petticoat. As usual she wore no bra and her nipples peered dumbly at the world, released from their confinement.

"Everything." Andy said. He turned to watch the effect on Atsuko. She licked her lips and her arms crossed over her chest as if to protect her tiny breasts. Natsumi dropped her tight skirt, then bent to remove panties and hose. The gaudy garters had dug slightly into her plump thighs, and contrasted with her plain white briefs. Still watching Atsuko, Andy slipped a finger down the crack of Natsumi's ass. His finger ended between the hair-rimmed lips of her cunt. He held her bent forward with one hand, stepped back and moved Natsumi around so her snatch was completely visible to Atsuko.

"Like it?" He asked. "It is the most beautiful thing in the world."

The girl said nothing but examined the rounded ass and parted purse lips with enthusiasm.

"Would you like to touch her?" Andy asked with a sneer. Atsuko shook her head.

"Andy-san!" Natsumi's complaining voice brought a grimace of lust to Andy's face.

"Undress me," he said, his eyes still on the dressed girl.

Natsumi did as she was bid, showing him off and by deft manipulation of his body, showing the other girl who was in charge. For a moment her head burrowed at his crotch, then she rose into his arms, kissing him deeply with demanding lips and tongue tasting of lipstick. Andy rubbed his body against hers and gripped her full ass, parting the mounds again. He closed his eyes for a moment, and opened them to see Atsuko leaning forward, her tongue sticking out of the side of her mouth. She straightened away when she caught his eyes on her, still saying nothing.

Grinning, Andy led Natsumi to the bed. She lay on it and Andy parted her legs as far apart as the could go. He knelt over her, then started stroking her body. His hands lingered on the dark tips of her breasts, on the hollows under her shoulders, then moved downwards. He tickled the deep well of her navel, then stroked against the almost-invisible scar of her appendectomy. Natsumi moved in protest as he knew she would. Andy found the slight scar beautifying, but knew she regarded it as ugly. Then finally he came to the junction of her legs. The black hair contrasted pleasingly with the brown skin. She raised her hips obligingly as he forced her up, bringing her strong mound into prominence. He looked up. Atsuko was peering abstractedly down at his fingers. There appeared to be a film of moisture on her lips.

Andy brought Natsumi's hand up between his legs. She cupped his balls, then began stroking the hardness of his lengthening rod. Atsuko's eyes caught the movement and she followed Natsumi's frigging hand as if hypnotized. Andy straddled Natsumi's head. His hands stroked the V of her belly, then parted the lips of her cunt exposing the pink inner lining. His loins descended until his balls were poised over Natsumi's face.

"Suck my balls," he commanded, staring into Atsuko's eyes. The thin girl's mouth was open and she was starting to pant. Natsumi opened her mouth and Andy could feel her warm breath blow against the hairs on his testicles. Then her warm mouth sucked in one of his stones and laved it with an expert tongue. She shifted to the other as he began penetrating her cunt with the four fingers of one hand while the other held her open. Gradually he increased his pressure, and the speed of his frigging fingers as she grew wetter and more aroused.

Atsuko moved about the bed impatiently, examining the action from all sides. She peered down at Natsumi's face, then examined Andy's ass minutely, all without touching them or herself. She bent near Andy's head and examine Natsumi's cunt clinically.

"Like it?" he whispered. She did not deign to answer.

Natsumi started moaning, at first with one of his balls in her mouth, then unconsciously, fighting for air between her legs. "No, you must not Andy-san. Please stop. Oh oh oh. Please, you must not do this. No Andy-san, no."

The speed of his hand motions increased as the sound of her voice reached him. He pinched her labia viciously and was rewarded by a contraction in the channel of her cunt and by an increase in her moans. He swung around on her body, kissing her roughly and running his hands over her slim body. She responded ardently to his kisses, running her hands over his body, feeling his erection and the muscles in his back and shoulders. Atsuko still looked on with interest but showed no intention of participating.

Andy rose from the supine woman. His cock stretched out erect before his belly. He turned to Atsuko to watch the effect of the male member on her. She was panting heavily, but made no move towards it. He moved towards her and she shrank back. He shrugged, causing the rod to dance and sway, then turned hurriedly back to Natsumi.

He rolled Natsumi over on her stomach and poised over her. Atsuko was sitting at the side of the bed. One of her hands was supporting her on the bed, the other was pressed hard into her lap. Andy knelt behind her and pushed her full buttocks apart. The tiny anal entrance winked at him. He had done this to Natsumi before, and knew she expected it. Andy spread her legs against her muted protests. He hurriedly slipped a cushion under her hips and then parted the golden globes of her ass again. The tiny brown ass hole beckoned. He could see that the lips below were glistening with moisture, and as usual his own lustfulness was exacerbated by Natsumi's continual teasing.

"No, please Andy-san. Not there. It is not right," she said as she felt his gaze upon her. "You must not bugger me." She used the English word, one he had taught her. "Don't do that. I am yours, do what you want. But not that. Stop. Please stop."

The knob of his cock pointed at the entrance and she could feel the crown rubbing against the flesh of her buns. Andy turned to Atsuko, now leaning over the scene of action. Her eyes were staring, hypnotized by the sight.

"Would you like to put it in for me?" crouching over Natsumi's ass he asked Atsuko. His cock was held in his fist, pointed downwards. The thin girl shook her head silently, but leaned forward to watch the procedure. Andy aimed his cock at the tiny rear bud, then placed the nose at the entrance. The muscular hole seemed to suck the tip in, and both Andy and Atsuko watched with fascination as the broad head parted the muscles and the shaft gradually followed. Natsumi squealed wordlessly and And rested for a moment, his balls against the slit of her cunt. Then he pulled out and set to work to fuck her. She called out in joy as he rose, then plunged into her again. This time there was no whining tone in her voice. "Wonderful! Wonderful" her eyes were closed to thick-lidded slits and Andy crouched over her, shafting her rapidly. She cried out in pleasure as the first wave of her orgasm reached her and clutched convulsively at the bed. Andy clenched his jaw, restraining himself as long as he could. He squeezed his eyes shut to enjoy the pressure of her muscular interior on his shaft. The juices were rising in his balls when he suddenly felt an imperious powerful hand squeeze the base of his scrotum. He almost screamed in pain and opened his eyes to see Atsuko, whom he had completely forgotten in the pleasure of Natsumi's behind, crouching on the bed. Her hands were on his cock and balls, and she looked at him silently with a fierce appeal. He struck out thoughtlessly, his blow landing strongly on her shoulder as pain lanced through his lions. She fell forward, her head to Natsumi's back. As she fell she pulled up her narrow skirt, exposing smooth buttocks encased in lacy bikini briefs.

"Like her," she mumbled. "Just like her."

Andy pulled out of Natsumi's rear. He scrambled around until he was posed behind Atsuko. Natsumi rolled over and caught the long-haired woman by the scruff of the neck. There was a look of anger on Natsumi's face and she forced Atsuko to bury her mouth into her musky dripping cunt. The artist slipped her tongue between Natsumi's hungry lower lips and began licking about with a will.

Andy slipped the briefs down, exposing the thin golden buttocks. He parted them and examined the tiny hole for a brief moment. Atsuko raised her head slightly against the pressure of Natsumi's hand. "Now!" she said in a muffled voice.

Andy rose over her, directing his slimy cock to her rear entrance. She cried out wordlessly, muffled by Natsumi's snatch, as the tip of his male lance widened the tight opening. Natsumi slapped her and simultaneously pulled her mouth deeper into her own opening. "She bit me!" she muttered in outrage, and then her eyes closed again as Atsuko renewed her lingual caress.

She was so tight Andy cried out in joy as his shaft slid into her rear hole. At last he found himself firmly in her. The pressure in his balls that had been building as he fucked Natsumi came to a boiling point. His hose squirted remorselessly into Atsuko's behind. She moaned something and moved herself back at him. He found her insides quivering as she joined him in a massive orgasm. He collapsed loosely onto her, and she flattened onto the bed under his weight. Only Natsumi's insatiable demand for use of her mouth forced Atsuko to continue moving. Andy panted heavily, his ass jerking faintly in the final throes of dying orgasmic peaks. Then Natsumi clutched at Atsuko's long hair and emitted a final wail of triumph and delight. For a long time after that the only motion was the heavy breathing, and the tiny motion of Andy's fingers as he stroked Atsuko's flanks.

"Why don't you join us in the bath?"

Atsuko nodded but made no move to rise. Andy shrugged and headed for the *furo*. Natsumi followed, admiring the slide of muscles in his ass and the sway of his glistening semi-soft cock. He squatted imperiously, turned on the *furo* heater, and Natsumi started soaping his back. Her hands stroked his limbs then descended inevitably to his crotch. The dark hairs raised a fine lather and as she soaped his cock, it rose too. She rinsed him off and he climbed into the tub. She smiled slightly and put on a full show as she washed herself thoroughly, enjoying his scrutiny as she rubbed lather into her breasts, under her armpits, between her legs and the rounded mounds of her ass. She washed herself off finally, tiring of the foreplay and climbed into the large tub. The water rose almost to their necks. As she descended she found herself being pierced by his stiff finger. The warm water penetrated her and she felt his finger shafting her while her own hands descended to his stiff cock, readying him for full penetration. Atsuko entered the bathroom and squatted by the high tub. She reached for the shower head and rinsed herself. Natsumi and Andy watched her thin body. She was almost scrawny, he decided. But the pleasure of the feel of her body against his was stills strong. He continued frigging Natsumi while wondering what Atsuko would do next.

She soaped herself, ignoring the couple in the tub completely. Her hands lingered with long lathered strokes over her belly and the inner level of her thighs. Then she parted the lips of her cunt with two fingers and dreamily soaped the insides. Her thin bony hips twitched, then moved faster and her eyes closed. A sudden quiver indicated the start of her orgasm. She parted the lips of her cunt and frigged at her clitoris, thrumming it like a frenzied guitar player. Suddenly her legs contracted and her thighs began quivering as her orgasm peaked. Gradually her motions slowed down. Her eyes opened, still blankly staring. She rinsed herself off then climbed into the bath. They made room for her, and she finally sat on top of both of them, soaking in blissful silence. Andy's hand stole around her and under her body. He started penetrating her cunt with his finger. She moved away, rose, and spread her legs facing Natsumi in mute demand, then bent forward presenting her thin buttocks to the man. Andy rose behind her and sought for her wet pussy with his hands. From below Natsumi's mouth sought the girl's tiny suspended breasts, then she licked at the water-dripping cunt. Andy presented his wet cock to her cunt. As Andy's shaft presented itself to Natsumi's lips from between the artist's legs, she licked at the passing lollipop, then confined herself to his balls as she shaft disappeared into the standing girl's body. The crown of his cock parted Atsuko's pussy. She cried out lightly as he penetrated her, sinking into the water and onto his erect cock as she did so. He clutched her small breasts, mauling them heedlessly as he jerked his prick deeper and deeper into her. She was extraordinarily tight and not well lubricated, but from the look on her face and the trembling of her body he knew she was enjoying the penetration, rough as it was. He was also conscious of Natsumi's mouth searching the crannies of Atsuko's exposed flower and the length of his male bag. He started to contract helplessly, his sperm emerging weakly into her body and they shook to and fro with the violence of his orgasm. As he started to subside into the water, Atsuko gave a sudden wordless cry and he felt her insides clenching on his softening prick. Natsumi pressed her face deeply to the other girl's, water lapping about her chin as they sank into the bath for the third time.

The thin pink cloud dispersed through the water and Atsuko nestled contentedly in his arms. The water buoyed her up and Andy, helped by Natsumi, easily jogged her up and down on his softening shaft.

"It was my first time," she said in a voice that was hardly over a whisper. Her fingers twined with Natsumi's and she returned the other girl's kiss ardently before turning to Andy.

At the door, after they had dressed to leave, Natsumi turned back for a second. "Am I still your steady?" she asked anxiously.

Andy grinned and pinched her rump. "Of course you are." He wondered what they both meant by the words.

CHAPTER 6

HOW YOU GOIN' TO KEEP THEM DOWN ON THE FARM. . . ?

"Again?"

The heavy lashed rather plump girl considered a moment with a smile. "Yes," she whispered and reached for her companion. Chieko Nakabe shifted to a more comfortable position, then changed her mind and swung herself onto her plumper lover's form. They kissed deeply, their lips mashed together into a red-on-red surface that moved with their passion. She rubbed her small sharp breasts against Mineko's plumper ones and one of her hands descended to the juncture of their legs. The touch of Mineko's crisp hair after still brought a tremor to her hands after all those months. She had waited so long for the touch of Mineko's bare body on her own, that now she could not have enough of her. Occasionally she regretted having had to use a trick to get between Mineko's legs. Jim Suzuki had been a good friend, helping in the seduction. She wondered what he was doing now, whether he had found as much happiness as she had over the past months.

Thought was banished as the pleasure of touching Mineko's skin started getting through to her. She slid down along the younger woman's body until her lips came into contact with the soft brush at the bottom of Mineko's smooth belly. She wet the line of velvety hairs that marked the start of the treasure she sought. Mineko spread her legs to ease her lover's access. Chieko slid further down, ignoring Mineko's half-hearted attempts to pull her around. Finally the plumper girl surrendered just as Chieko reached the upper end of the delicious split between her legs.

She gently parted the plump outer lips exposing the coral cleft inside. Mineko's inner lips were as delicate as the rest of her cunt. The clitoris was a tiny pearl hidden within the folds, and Chieko headed for it unerringly. Her experienced tongue licked out and moistened the button once more, and then she started a licking and sucking motion that soon drove Mineko wild. She clutched at Chieko's head, forcing the delicious lips to come into stronger contact with her own. She could barely control the motion of her pelvis which trembled with the waves of pleasure that ran through her.

Then Chieko changed her tactics. She opened the sweet cunt as wide as she could, fully exposing the interior pink tissues and the deep tight little hole. She could see it was fully lubricated by now. Her tongue protruded, as stiff as she could make it, and she stabbed deeply into the waiting hole. She could barely hear Mineko's delighted scream because the warm thighs clamped over her head. Forcefully she moved her head up and down, driving the lingual cock as deeply as she could into Mineko, then rubbing the tip of her nose forcefully into the sweet button at the head of the slit. She felt Mineko's passion rising, and the quivering turned to a forceful writhing that almost dislodged her. Chieko waited for some of the orgasmic tremors to subside, then pulled away from the embracing legs. She quickly reversed herself, her thighs surrounding Mineko's head, and began licking the entire length of the slit, from the pearly clitoris she held exposed with her fingers, to the tiny anal button. As she felt Mineko respond, and as her movements turned more rapid, she could not help wondering if Jim had had his cock inside Mineko's ass. She had always refused to admit it to

Chieko, even when the older woman had admitted she had had Jim there.

Mineko watched delightedly as Chieko's crotch descended to her face. Impatiently she slid her hands over the thinner woman's buttocks, pried the thighs apart and brought the musky smelling treasure to her mouth. Chieko's cunt sported a full brush of hair which was more impressive than her own. Mineko pulled forcefully at her lover's buttocks, then sucked hungrily at the wet soft tissues, engulfing full lips and sweet-smelling hairs into her mouth. She was rewarded for her energetic sucking by a swiveling motion of Chieko's hips. Pulling slightly back she parted the full buns and delighted herself by a full examination of Chieko's crotch. She buried herself again in the warm welcoming depths between her lover's legs, trying to emulate her by stiffening her tongue and fucking Chieko lingually. Then she drew back again to examine the result. The clenched starfish of Chieko's ass hole caught her attention and she examined it minutely, even touching the tight moist tissues with her finger. She wondered hazily what it would be like, having an object, say a man's cock, shoved into there. The thought naturally brought back memories of her first, and so far only man. Jim Suzuki had blackmailed her into sleeping with him, but she did not regret it for one moment. Her only regret was that he was not here at the very moment. At the thought she began fantasizing what she would do with him. Suddenly she found herself responding wildly to Chieko's tongue on her twat, imagining it to be Jim's cock. Her own mouth sought Chieko's vagina with increasing demand, as if she were kissing Jim. She felt the start of her second orgasm coinciding with the flush of moisture from Chieko as her lover responded to her fierce ardor. The two women collapsed side by side, still stroking and licking one another. Then Chieko crawled up beside Mineko and rested the plumper girl's head softly against her breast. Mineko tickled the still-prominent nipple, knowing they would be both ready again in a short while, enjoying the peace and security of her lover. Nonetheless, the image of Jim, his cock fully erect, pursued her in her imagination.

Mineko pulled away from her lover and rose to one elbow. The older woman's face was more relaxed than it had been earlier. Being a businesswoman and helping her husband expand and run his business had taken their toll on Chieko. Mineko stroked the dear face. She remembered when Chieko had arrived as a new bride. The bones of her face had been hidden by a layer of smooth flesh which had made her face seen almost broad. But after almost a year of toiling at a business she had made her own, of behaving like a proper daughter-in-law and wife, tiredness had etched sharp lines in the older woman's face. She knew Chieko had not taken so much as one day off since her wedding. And indeed, the Nakabe Electronics Emporium had flourished, due partly to Nakabe's technical expertise, partly to Chieko's business acumen. Mineko kissed her lightly, and Chieko responded hungrily. She laughed low in her throat. That hunger never seemed satisfied. It was like . . . it was like Jim's. At the thought of the young man Mineko's eyes clouded. She thought of the pleasure of his embrace, of the delight of being with him. Even his treachery and his betrayal of her into Chieko's arms did not matter compared to the delight she felt in his company. She sighed slightly, her full breasts bobbing over the older woman's face, then straightened up in the motel bed. She realized she had made up her mind long before, but it had come to her clearly only now.

"I must go to Tokyo." Mineko looked down onto Chieko's thin face.

"Aren't you happy with me?" the older woman cried.

"Of course I am," dear Chieko. But I, . . ." she blushed, "I must know if my feelings for Jimmu-san are real and deep. I miss him . . ."

"He's probably found another woman by now. And forgotten you completely." Chieko said cruelly. Tears started in her eyes.

"Why not come with me?" Mineko said excitedly. The

sight of Chieko, who had always been the stronger of the two, crying her eyes out was one she found hard to bear "After all, you found pleasure in him too."

"I cannot leave my husband!" Chieko said in shock.

"Just for a time," Mineko said contritely. "You do need a holiday."

The idea had never occurred to Chieko. Once married to Nakabe, she had devoted herself to his benefit and his interests. And as Mineko had said, she did need a holiday, time to gather energy. "Yes," she said suddenly. "I will go too But I cannot go now. The summer gift season is not over yet. There is much to do in the store. You go now, and I will come to Tokyo some other time. Let me kiss you again." She rolled Mineko around, then slipped lower down her hard belly, towards the juicy expanse of her cunt. her Red tongue slipped in and out, leaving a trail of delicious moisture across the pale brown skin.

Tokyo was awesome, Mineko felt. She had thought it would be no different from Nagoya, the only large city she had been in before, but Tokyo just seemed to go on and on, row of grey wooden houses interspersed by occasional blocks of apartments. She had not called Jim, though that would have been appropriate. She was apprehensive about meeting him, and the apprehension was combined with anticipation. He was the first man to have been in her, in fact, the only one. Since he had deflowered her by a trick some months before, she had been occupied solely with Chieko, to the exclusion of male company. Her parents were urging her to marry, had actually suggested several eligible young men, but she had turned them all down well before the important and irreversible *omiai* stage when she and any prospective husband would be introduced to one another formally.

Now here she was in Tokyo, following her own heart. Or was it that sweet organ Chieko was constantly extolling which lay well below her heart? She shrugged mentally, just as the organ in question seemed flooded with juices at the thought of seeing Jim again.

It was dark by the time she ascended from the subway and managed to find her way to the address Jim had given her. It was a small apartment building overlooking a busy shopping street. She debated for a long time before entering the lobby and scanning the address boxes. Her heart started pounding again, and she wondered whether she had made a mistake, then saw the little sign saying ANDREW MIDDLER-JIM SUZUKI. As she rode the elevator up she abruptly raised her skirt and felt her own crotch. Her panties were sopping wet, and she knew at that moment that the decision was made for her. She paused for only a moment at the door to the apartment, then rang the bell. Somehow she knew Jim would be there. She found that her nervous fingers were undoing the upper buttons of her one-piece dress.

There was no answer to her ring. She rang the bell again, then again, to no avail. Saddened she turned to go just as she heard steps on the floor inside and someone began fumbling at the door. She turned. Jim was silhouetted against the light that filtered through the apartment from the street. His hair was tousled and he wore a loose *yukata* robe. She threw herself forward with a glad cry. Her arms went around him and her lips crushed his. Dazed from what appeared to be a nap, he reached for the *genkan* light. She stopped him, stepping into the apartment and closing the door behind her.

"No, no," she managed to choke out. "Later, if you wish. Just now I need you in me. Feel how wet I am." She led his hands between her legs and he rubbed the wet nylon. She feared suddenly that he would reject her, and growing bold she shushed his mouth as he began to speak. "No matter. Even if you want me the other way, from behind, as you said last time. Yes, any way at all. Don't speak now, just accept me."

She fell to her knees and searched out his maleness from under the robe. He was erect and hard, the shaft smooth to the touch as she rubbed it to her cheeks then kissed it inexpertly as she pulled down her panties and hose and leaned forward.

"Now, please," she begged. "Please do not disappoint me."

The last appeal was more than he could take. He crouched over her and she felt his cock penetrate her waiting female flesh, covered by her lubricating oils. Then the male head withdrew, and she held her breath, awaiting the answer to her invitation.

The cock head pecked at her clenched anus and she sighed aloud. "I am so sorry I rejected your offer last time, my dear. Take me now. Have it, for you only." For a moment it withdrew and she feared he would reject her as much as she had feared that he would accept. Then she felt something cool on her anus and knew he was being kind. He was anointing her rear with some unguet. She wondered if he kept the jelly there for this particular use and a spasm of envy and jealousy spurted through her. Then the jealousy was swamped by the unfamiliar touch of his finger probing strongly at her rear. She shifted on her knees, opening her buttocks and sticking them out to facilitate his entry. One of his other fingers sought out the tiny delectable source of her pleasure and tickled her clitoral bud. She was conscious of his finger worming its way into her rear canal. The slight pain she felt at first soon gave way to pleasure as he continued diddling her pearl. She felt herself moisten, and at that moment was ready, even eager to accept what she had seen to that point as a necessary sacrifice for her love. She heard the sound of someone moaning and suddenly realized that is was herself. The finger was inserted in her to the knuckle, smoothing and slicking the rear entrance way. She was completely relaxed now, and waited expectantly as the probing digit was withdrawn. He bent behind her in the dimness, pulling her smooth buttocks apart with his hands. She knew he was contemplating the scene, and she hoped it did not disgust him. She enjoyed looking at women's cunts, at least one cunt, her lover Chieko's. But she had never dared examine Chieko as frankly as she was being examined now.

She felt him place two kisses, nibbling slightly, on the protruding mounds of her buttocks, then he was looming over her, one hand on the small of her back. The tip of his cock nose against the furrow between her thighs, then orient towards the tiny waiting bud, all slick with the work of his finger. He pushed inside, gradually widening the entrance. She stretched painfully, but bore it with fortitude that turned to acceptance and love as he nibbled at her back and the nape of her neck, whispering wordlessly. When she was distended as far as she thought it could go, the pressure eased as the flanges of his cock slid through the guarding portal muscles. She exhaled gratefully, and he paused to allow her time to adjust to his presence.

It was Mineko who took the initiative, slowly and gradually settling herself back onto his man root, hoping to take him in completely. He held her hips lightly, occasionally stroking her flanks or squeezing her pendant breasts, encouraging her on without forcing himself into her. At last she felt her buttocks resting completely against the hairs at the base of his muscular belly. She waited there passively, only oscillating her bum slightly to keep up the friction. Daringly she sent a hand along her belly until she could feel his ball bag, tracing the length of it to the entrance to her own anus. She was thrilled by the perverse pleasure of it, a man actually inserted into her ass.

Now he started moving into her. Gently at first, then with greater vigor. She sighed again, this time with more pleasure as he gradually increased the speed of his actions. The pleasure grew as he began strumming the waiting erect bud at the entrance to her vulva. Finally she cried out in triumph as she felt the first hints of her own growing passion overcoming the pain and rising towards a climax. She rested her head on the *tatami* then extended her arms backwards. His muscular ass was contracting and hardening as he forced himself into her anal regions. She clutched hard at the muscular flesh, digging her nails as deeply into him as she could. He bit her neck and shoulders, ramming himself uncaring into her. She welcomed the slight pain and felt her cunt contract, then his fingers dipped into the empty hole and seemed to fill a gap in her life. It was so good, so good to feel him in both her holes at once. A small orgasm shivered through her tissues, then another. She knew she was building up to a climax she had never reached before. She wished Jim had two cocks, to fill her completely. She wished she could see the pleasure on his face as he fucked her behind.

The outside door opened abruptly and Mineko craned around in surprise. She screamed. Jim was standing there, framed by the doorway, dressed in a dark business suit. She twisted her head around some more in panic as he closed the door. The face peering into into her own was Jim's, . . . and yet that of a *gaijin*. Her mouth opened in shock as Jim took a step forward. He smiled, and blush started to suffuse her face. She wanted to move, wanted to eject this intruder from her behind, yet was paralyzed by embarrassment.

"I see you've met my brother Andy."

She tried to say "Brother?" but no sound came from her lips, they just opened and closed.

"Won't you join us?" the man in her ass asked mischievously.

The briefcase dropped from Jim's hand as he closed the door. His pants were next, and Mineko suddenly found herself rolled over on the *tatami* until the man in her ass was under her. She raised her head passively, resigned, even curious about the outcome. The male cock was still lodged into her behind and Jim knelt between her legs. She found his cock nuzzling her unoccupied cunt lips, and then he was sinking deeply into her, filling her as she had never been filled before. She cried out in gratified surprise, then spread herself more to accommodate both male members as they set to work at her front and behind. This was what she had wanted, she knew as her arms went around

Jim's shoulders. She clawed at him as his cock sought the heart of her pleasure. The new freshness of his attack on her cunt overcame the smouldering embarrassment she had felt momentarily. She pulled his head to her and sank her tongue into his willing mouth. He pounded into her, and Andy almost suffocating yet still game, responded by arching his hips at the two of them from below. She squealed aloud as the first shock of a massive orgasm ripped through her. Her hands flashed from one man to another, unable to find any difference in the two bodies. She explored the juncture of her legs, touching the two cocks that sprouted and rooted within her. Closing her eyes again she surrendered to the sensation, and was barely conscious of the flood of sperm that leaked out between her legs from both sides as her men erupted into her.

They rolled over to one side on the sweet-smelling *tatami* mats. Their softening cocks were still held in by her demanding holes. She smiled shyly at Jim, then turned back to include Andy. he kissed her lightly and she turned back to Jim. "You do have two cocks. Just what I was wishing for," she said. There was no trace of self-consciousness in her now, and Jim smiled, understanding what she meant.

"I missed you so much," Mineko admitted, lying with her face buried in Jim's chest. Andy was lazily stroking her soft behind and kissing her shoulders. "You are sure you are not jealous?"

"Jealous?" Jim asked in surprise. "I am so pleased you found my brother enjoyable you have no idea. As a matter of fact, I think it is wonderful." He bent forward and kissed her mouth. "How long will you be in Tokyo?"

"Not too long. I must get back to my job, to my parents. They want me to get married," she sadly. "I would like to stay, to be near you, but that is impossible. The day after tomorrow I must go."

"You can stay here then." he said. "How is Nakabe Chieko, by the way?" he asked her mischievously.

Mineko started to blush, then smiled. her eyes were

sparkling. ''She was supposed to come with me, but could not. We were planning to come together, she on business, I for the shopping, but she could not. Poor woman, she needs the holiday. She has been working too hard.''

''Ah, . . . How are relations between you?'' Jim asked cautiously.

''They are wonderful!'' Mineko said, her eyes shining. ''I love her so much. Not as I love you of course . . .''

''She can stay here too, when she comes,'' Andy said. Jim had described his relationship with Chieko, and he wanted to see for himself. he mentally licked his chops.

''Oh no, she could not. She is coming to Tokyo partly on business, partly to shop, and she will need to stay at a hotel. As I should.''

''There is no reason you cannot spend some time here, though?'' Jim asked. There was a tinge of disappointment in his voice.

''Of course I will, my love,'' she cupped his cheeks in her palms. ''And so will Chieko, I know. And I won't be jealous, in fact. . . .'' She blushed and lowered her eyelashes. Andy laughed behind her back, then pulled regretfully out of her warm hole. Jim did the same.

''In fact, you have caught us in the middle of moving to a new place. He waved a hand at the boxes and bundles. ''The movers are arriving tomorrow. You can consider it your home.''

''Your business must be succeeding then,'' she said as Jim tweaked her nipple.

''It is indeed,'' Andy said.

CHAPTER 7

AND YOU TOO, A BRUTE

"I have come back." Matsuko Baba said the formal phrases with something of an emphasis, and she regarded them with the gravity that was her hallmark. She was dressed conservatively as usual, and carried a heavy bag without any sign of apparent effort.

"It is very nice of you to have arrived to visit us," Jim said formaly but in a joking tone as he ushered her into the new house.

"It is nothing," she said the polite phrase automatically. "Though we have not finished my education. May I sit down?"

"Of course." She regarded them both gravely, then reached out with a fat arm and stroked the bulges in their pants. Her demeanor was placid, but there was something demanding and fiery in her eyes.

"I have just noticed recently," she said, "that Japanese men are addicted to violence."

Jim laughed, saw the expression on her face, and apologized. "I just thought it was the understatement of the year. I mean, look at the films, TV samurai movies, comic books. . . ."

"And pornographic magazines," she said seriously, opening her large bag. She extracted several glossy magazines. Most of them were devoted to the tying art of *hojo jutsu* in its erotic version. There were pictures of women tied in a variety of postures, suspended from ceilings, lying on floors, couches, beds.

''I find them disgusting,'' Jim said. He had took no exception to people enjoying themselves as they liked, and had discovered a streak of sadism in his own nature, but the pictures she had brought. . . . The women were tied up in a variety of uncomfortable postures. Not mere strings, but thick white ropes in complicated arrangements and impressive knots bound them to themselves, to others, to frames which held or suspended them in the air.

''Did you know there are several studios where men can photograph models dressed like this?'' she inquired mildly.

''Horribly uncomfortable,'' Andy said. ''I imagine they are paid a lot.''

''It is possible my future husband would like to do this. I want you to prepare me.''

''You're getting married?'' Andy inquired. Jim was preoccupied in looking at the pictures. They were humiliating, and evoked both revulsion and fascination in him.

''No, but my father is already making rumblings in that direction, and I imagine it will become necessary. He will probably find someone. I am quite plain,'' she said frankly, regarding him earnestly, ''but rather rich, and from a good family.'' She dismissed the mater as unimportant.

Andy picked up a magazine and examined the pictures carefully. ''I can't tie you up like this. These knots are works of art. I mean, the Japanese excel in knots, but even so, these. . . .''

''That is not a problem. First, I have brought you a guide.'' She fished in her gigantic bag once more and procured a large, traditionally bound volume. THE ART OF KNOTS it said on the spine in gilt Chinese characters. Inside it contained page after page of illustrations and demonstrations of knot tying. From the relatively simple art of tying gifts, to the complex knots needed for tying parts of armor, tea-caddy coverings, and religious hangings. It was a beautiful book, and Jim devoured it hungrily with his eyes.

"This is actually just a gift, though you might get some ideas from it. But tying these precise knots is not necessary. All I want is to be tied somehow. And of course, to be beaten."

Her calm was somehow terrifying. "Why did you come to us then?" Jim asked uneasily.

"Because I can tell you to stop. I know I can rely on you. My future husband, on the other hand, would be under no compulsion to do what *I* want, to stop when *I* say. And within limits I could not refuse him. This way I have more control over the situation," she said candidly.

The two men looked at one another blankly, then smiled weakly.

"Your bed or my *futon*?" Jim asked.

"We'll alternate," Andy replied.

"Good," she said, then delved into her bag again, producing lengths of smooth silken cord. "I went to the *noshente* shop in Iidabashi. Did you know they made cords for armour? Very strong, very smooth."

They looked at her in some perplexity as she shrugged matter-of-factly out of her clothes. Her chunky, almost fat body stirred them to action.

"Let's fuck you first," Jim suggested. He was stripping as he did so and his natural exuberance infected Andy as well. She studied them as they stripped, enjoying the feeling of two men obeying *her* orders. They rushed at her and she fended them off, laughing loudly as they pulled her to the floor.

"No," she whispered. "Tie me up!"

They reached together for the cords and started binding her limbs inexpertly. Perversely, she shrugged out of the knots. She experienced a spurt of anger at the two men. These *gaijin* were hopeless at some things.

"This is what I want to try," she said, pointing to one of the illustrations. The young woman, far lighter than

Matsuko, had been suspended from the beams of what appeared to be a traditional warehouse or other storage area. Her arms and legs were in the air, her head hung down, and her ass was sticking out. Andy looked at the picture, then at Matsuko, at the beam over the doorway. The wall between the exposed decorative beam and the ceiling was actually a panel of pierced wood. Like the *fusuma* sliding door which ran under the beam, the panel was removable, to privide more ventilation in the hot days of summer. He knew Japanese carpentry was solid, but Matsuko was no featherweight. She gave them no time to reconsider. Her busy hands were quickly tying several of the thick cords she had brought into intricate patterns. Jim watched her flying fingers. He had noticed before that the Japanese seemed to have an instinctive, almost unconscious knowledge of knots. The youngest child or oldest farmer could tie a complex and elegant knot without the slightest effort or forethought. And yet, when he or any other foreigner tried what seemed to be a simple tie, the thing looked as if a particularly messy troll had been at work.

Matsuko rose to her feet, magnificently naked. She showed them how to tie her to the loops she had made. Andy sliped out the upper panel and opened the doors. He threw the cords she had knotted over the beam, then tugged at the loops. Matsuko looked on with approval. Following the picture they raised her in the air, then slipped the loops over her limbs and tightened them. She held the soft cords with her hands. She found it was uncomfortable but bearable. Her long hair hung down almost to the floor. She looked at the two naked men from an uncomfortable angle. Their cocks were soft and she snorted with annoyance.

"How does it feel?" Andy asked with concern.

She did not reply. Jim was staring at her ass. He was stroking his cock which was rising smoothly to an erection. She ignored Andy and watched Jim with approval. "Smack my behind," she whispered. Jim seemed absorbed in a world of his own. "Jimmu-san!" her voice was a whiplash. She did not know how long she would be able to tolerate her position, and wanted to make the most of it. "Hit my ass," she implored.

He bent down to explore her first. Her full buttocks were squeezed together and the entire length of her almost hairless slit was compressed and available for his gaze and touch. He ran the side of his hand along the lit, dipping into the compressed holes. She was dry, not yet ready. His hands descended to her handbag and he searched the insides, extracting her lipstick which he smeared liberally over her exposed outer cunt lips. Then he struck.

Matsuko screamed helplessly. The blow had been so sudden and so painful she was unable to control her response. Jim peered at her in surprise.

"Go on!" she called. "Don't stop. I must feel."

He smacked her again, softer this time. Andy looked on bemused at the sight of his brother and the bound woman. Jim's hand rose and fell and Matsuko's full, everted buttocks flushed rosily. Jim's cock was an erect throbbing spear. He rose to his full height, parted the compressed lips of her cunt with his thumbs then pulled her to his stiff glowing pole.

Her cunt was tighter than it had ever been. Jim forced himself thoughtlessly into her, ignoring her whimpers of pain. His cock disappeared between the mounds of her thighs. The plump outer lips of her femininity seemed to follow the shaft into her warm soft interior. The red lipstick stained his cock as he pushed her away from him.

Using Matsuko as a pendulum, Jim began rocking her on and off his cock. At first the motion and the insertion were painful and uncomfortable, but gradually the pleasure increased and the friction of his cock against her squeezed cunt overrode the discomfort of her stretched limbs. Matsuko's head dropped and her hair swept almost to the floor. She caught Andy staring at her doubtfully. Upside-down, his face looked goblin-like. He was stroking his cock which had now come fully erect. Opening her mouth wordlessly in invitation, she made sucking motions with her lips. As if sleepwalking, Andy moved forward and inserted his cock into her mouth. She sucked him in, softening her lips and using her tongue. She could feel his cock filling her mouth. Softening her throat she let the knob slide down until Jim pulled her back, impaling her by her pussy to his hard frame. Then as he pushed her forwards she felt Andy's cock slipping down her throat. She found herself in a dreamy, helpless state. The pain in her arms and ankles from the ropes was still there. She felt disoriented, vaguely dizzy, and the male pricks inserted in her were gradually raising her lust to a dreamy height she did not know existed.

Andy and Jim clutched at her, bringing themselves closer, immobilizing her suspended form between them. Andy looked down at her, then pulled back. Matsuko's face was purpling and he could hear snoring sounds from her throat. He pulled back carefully and her head swung free. Jim, his face a mask went on thrusting into her.

"Jim!" Andy called, slapping him roughly on the shoulder.

Jim opened his eyes, Andy near panic, was staring at Matsuko's purpling face and slack lips. He withdrew from her hurriedly. "Hold her up!" Andy, panicked and staring, did not respond until Jim called to him again. They raised her body, lowered the ropes from the beam, and quickly pulled them off her. Jim felt for her pulse, then quickly started artificial respiration. The blood retreated from her face and her breathing returned to normal. She opened her eyes and looked dazedly at the two men.

She sipped the water gratefully, propped up between them. Her ass was still stinging from Jim's blows, but perplexedly she seemed pleased by the ordeal.

"Never again," Jim said.

"Nothing happened," she said mildly.

"Never again," he insisted, "Promise us you'll never do that. Not even if your husband to be, whoever the lucky son-of-a-bitch is, wants it."

Pleased by the concern in the two men's faces, she smiled brightly at them. "I promise. Now," she added briskly, "We have not finished."

They stared at her dumbly as she indicated the ropes once again.

"Jimmu-san, you have a *shinai*," she said. It was more an order than a question.

"He looked at her, horrified. "I don't know where it is," he said weakly.

"Go and find it!" she snapped. Growing up a spoiled only daughter had its advantages, as she knew. At the very least it had taught her to command. He cowered away as she turned to Andy.

Five minutes later Jim returned, having unearthed the bamboo practice sword among the pile of Andy's things they had yet to unpack. Matsuko was bound into a bundle on the bed. Her hands had been tied behind her back, her feet tied loosely to her wrists. She was gagged with a white folded cloth. One of the open magazines on the bed explained how Andy had been able to do it. Andy looked at the *shinai*. "She wants you to use it on her ass," he said.

"Are you sure?" Jim was still uneasy. His hands on the kidskin covered hilt were sweaty.

Matsuko glared at him over her shoulder and nodded her head vigorously. Jim looked at the flushed behind. There was a tightness at the pit of his stomach and he knew his breathing was shallow and uneven. Matsuko squirmed on the bed and mumbled into the gag. He raised the *shinai*. The split bamboo whistled through the air and fell down with a crash on her smooth fat buttocks. Jim knew that the sound was largely the effect of the four split bamboo lathes crashing against one another. Nonetheless, he also knew that the bamboos stung: he had been hit often enough at *kendo* practice during the few months he had been able to put up with it. Mechanically he raised the *shinai* again. She squealed against the gag as he hit her several more times then let the fencing sword drop.

Her posterior was blazing a ripe red, and some of the stripes were oozing blood. Hardly knowing what he was doing Jim flung himself upon her. His hands stroked the outraged surfaces and he kissed her thoroughly. Then his hands, taking off on their own opened her buttocks and exposed the length of her purse. The slipery lips were flushed. The brown starfish of her ass was clenching and relaxing rhythmically with hger breathing. The black hairs that fringed her lower lips were moist, clinging to the surface of her thighs. He pulled back, his cock was made of molten steel and he stabbed it deep into her waiting female crevice. Matsuko shrieked wildly as the hairs at the base of his cock scraped painfully against her lacerated flesh. Jim pumped into her carelessly, and she cried out again and again in abandon. He pulled suddenly out of her as he felt his balls jerk into their preliminary throes. Rolling her around he pointed his cock at her face and milked the length of his shaft. Gobs and strings of cream ejaculated from the tip and struck her full in the face. He did it again and again until he was completely empty.

Matsuko felt the pain dimly. It was bearable, even when Jim roughly thrust himself into her and rubbed against her painful rear. She enjoyed the opportunity to be completely inhibited, and her screams were only partly from the pain, largely an expression of lack of inhibitions. She watched with interest as Jim's cock spewed into her face. She would have liked to taste him. Suddenly though she was distracted as Andy grabbed her hips and parted her still-stinging buttocks. He pulled her full figure to him, rutting between the large soft mounds. His first jab found her tight anus and she resisted it as well as she could. He slapped her buttocks furiously as Jim spurted over her face, and she relaxed the tension allowing him into her tight posterior. Then he pulled out and sought her other entrance. She resisted him again to the best of her ability and he rained blows on her buttocks and hips, grinding his fingers into her snatch and the crack of her ass. Fully inserted in her he rutted about, barely pulling out his shaft before jamming it in again.

Matsuko screamed without restraint at the pain of his hands on her bruised ass, but the pleasure was starting to rise in her as well. Andy shafted her again and again, changing his target as he did so. She screamed unreservedly into the gag, but now it was from pleasure. The pain was completely unnoticed, subsumed into a growing awareness of her own skin and flesh. She wished she could tell them to untie her, so that she could hold the man to her. Instead she felt the rising tide of her own need, the feel of unbridled sexuality and lust wash over her. She creamed at him, her insides rippling with the power of her senses and the contraction of her muscles. And then a sweet darkness enfolded her as the last dregs of pleasure sent sparks through the entire volume of her body. She was completely unconscious when seconds later, Andy slumped over her form, his hips pumping the last of his juices into her.

Matsuko lay on Andy's bed in the last stages of pleased sexual languor. After untying her unconscious form the two men had massaged her limbs gently, rubbing in some skin oil they had found in her bag. She had thought of everything. She was touched and pleased by their consideration, and looked at both of them fondly. Relieved, they nestled besides her.

"What now?" she asked brightly.

Jim gulped. He was not sure they were up to anything else.

"I have an idea," Andy said. "A woman."

Matsuko looked into space, tasting the idea in her mind, then she smiled fully. "That would be nice."

CHAPTER 8

RUNNING BEFORE A WIND

The ringing phone shattered a quiet evening. Andy reached for the phone while still juggling figures in his head. Jim reached for it while trying to decide whether he could muster the energy to find a disco or bar.

"*Moshi moshi*?" They both heard a vaguely familiar female voice. "May I speak to Andzy-san or Jimmu-san?"

"This is he," they both said simultaneously.

"Kitamura *sacho* would like to speak to you please."

"Wonder what the dad wants?" Jim spoke into the phone.

"I guess to congratulate us on the new house," Andy answered smugly.

"Andy? Jim?" a cheerful voice boomed into their ears. "How are you boys? Congratulations on your new home. *Omedeto*. I am sorry we cannot come to see you. . . ."

"Too busy," admitted a milder, more subdued voice which almost whispered into their ears. Jim and Andy both grinned. Leonard Fine was very much quieter than his friend, partner, and co-father Kitamura Dansuke. "We're sending Mayumi to you with something. . . ."

"A job," Kitamura bellowed into their ears. "I have a job for Jim. Mayumi will tell you all about it when she arrives. I need a program analyzed."

Andy kept silence while Jim asked some technical questions, to which Kitamura, professing ignorance of computers, had no reply. Nor did Fine, though he was the scientist of the pair. "Just analyze the tape, any way you can," Fine instructed. "Mayumi is carrying them. She should be there sometime later this day. Treat her right, ne?" They all laughed. Mayumi was an old friend and a favorite of both younger men.

Mayumi was a vision of loveliness. For the occasion she had put on some makeup, something they knew she rarely did. Her short hair was brushed to glossy perfection, and her petite figure was encased in an expensive light dress that clung to her body demonstrating to any who cared to look that she did not need, nor want, any undergarments in the heat of summer.

"Much better than the lab coat," Andy joked.

She laughed and brandished an imaginary syringe, lunging towards Jim's thigh. he laughed too and caught her in his arms, though she struggled free easily. Among her many talents, she was a first class biochemist, and an adept at a new and revolutionary martial art that Lenny Fine and "Kitty" Kitamura, the boys' fathers had been developing over the years.

"First we have some business to dispose of," she said seriously, smoothing her dress. Andy grinned, noticing how the short tussle with Jim had erected her prominent nipples.

She opened her bag and extracted two items. The first was a small crystal phial with a large stopper. The second was a flat plastic disk, of the kind for carrying tape reels.

"Are you sure you should be walking around with that?" Jim said nervously. He pointed to the vial.

"If that's what I think it is, you're running one hell of a risk," Andy added.

"No. Please don't worry. This is a new product. We call it SuccSex. It only contains some dilute SP-15. The sample concentrate is for delivery to the Tokyo manufacturing plant. It is the tape that is important. For you, Jimmu-san.''

''What's in it? Kitty didn't want to say over the phone.'' he asked.

''This is the manufacturing control for the pheromone. The manufacturing process is supposed to be completely automatic for obvious reasons. We can't afford to have the workers constantly trying to jump on any person of the opposite sex passing by. Unfortunately, the programmer who wrote it, a brilliant man, died of a heart attack some days ago. Fine-san suggested that you try to decode it. Its full of ah software traps, he said. I'm afraid neither he nor I, nor for that matter anyone on our staff, is any good with advanced computer analysis.'' Leonard Fine was either Andy's or Jim's father or both. he was a brilliant chemist, specializing in scents, and had developed a human sex pheromone —SP 15—whose effects Jim and Andy had already experienced. Used by itself the pheromone was deadly, leaving nothing in human minds but an urge to copulate. used in dilute amounts, sold in perfume it would cut all the competition in the perfume business off at the knees.

''I'm flattered,'' Jim answered, taking the tape gingerly. ''But I need more information. Have any idea what computer language this was written in? And what machine? I asked Lenny but he was far from sure. How can anyone so brilliant be so ignorant?''

''He's an intuitive genius, like me, machine-mind,'' Andy taunted his brother.

''There is a note there with all the information we have,'' she said soothingly. ''The president did not want to speak on it over the phone.''

Andy picked up the phial. It was of crystal, beautifully cut. A label bore the usual Clouds and Rain logo, a picture of the company headquarter-mansion. Superimposed over it in tiny gold letters was one word: ''**SuccSex**.'' An additional label in Japanese emphasized that this was an industrial sample, not for distribution, and not to be opened incautiously.

"Don't open it," Mayumi cautioned. "The pheromone is very dilute, but this is still an industrial strength material."

Andy leered at her. "Not even to put a drop on you? Just for scientific reasons. To test its efficacy?"

She grinned back. "It is much more subtle than the ointment I used on you when we first met. . . ."

"That was naughty of you," Jim joined the conversation, raising his head from the notes and the tape. "You had us immobilized."

She giggled in reply, hiding her mouth behind her hand.

Jim and Andy looked at one another speculatively, then stared at Mayumi. The slim dark-haired girl backed away from the two men in pretended alarm. They advanced upon her, frowning sternly until her giggles made them break out in laughter.

"We must immobilize this infernal mad scientist, O super crime fighter," Andy said in a sepulchral voice.

"I, the Green Hornet, will proceed to do so at once." Jim leaped for the girl, she fled towards the door, still giggling. Andy intercepted her.

"No one can evade the Shadow!" he exclaimed triumphantly as she tripped him deftly and they fell to the *tatami* in a tangle of limbs. Jim joined the pileup and they fought breathlessly on the yielding mats. Finally she was immobilized, Jim sitting gently on her feet, Andy holding her squirming hands.

"Doctor, to the examination table!" Andy declared, then he bent over Mayumi and kissed her red mouth. She responded fiercely, still struggling to release her hands. The two men picked her up bodily and headed for Andy's room.

"Oh, no, help, I'm being kidnapped," she squealed in a high falsetto as she saw the bed. Jim released her and hurried away while Andy controlled the squirming girl with his hands and mouth, nibbling away at her ears and provoking a fresh cascade of giggles. Jim returned with a handful of stockings. "I knew Matsuko had left some her stuff," he declared triumphantly.

Mayumi was soon bound to the bed legs, spread on the sheet like a dark skirted angle. Her short skirt had to be hiked up to allow for the spread of her legs. She watched the two men, anticipating the next act in their play.

"Let us test the mad scientist's nefarious preparation. On herself!" Andy leered.

"No! You must not," she said, showing the first signs of real alarm. "it will be wasted!"

"Only two drops love?" Andy reassured her, asking her permission at the same time.

She smiled. "Very well, only two drops."

The bulky stopper of the tiny phial unscrewed displaying a drop dispenser built in: all SP products were too powerful to permit accidental spilling.

Jim held up the tiny bottle. "When the sun touches the masthead," he declaimed in sepulchral tones, "the virgin will be sacrificed."

She giggled again "I've *never* been a virgin before. But where's the masthead?"

"Here!" Andy declared. He had slipped off his clothes and now stood, his half-erect prick being brought to life by a gentle stroking motion. She watched the soft shaft and the hairy bag beneath and grinned lustfully, then raised her hips as far as she could from the bed, teasing the two men.

"We cannot leave her this way, O grand priest," Andy said. "My knife will not penetrate her armor!"

"Your knife does seem to be too blunt for any real action," Jim commented, looking at Andy's soft penis. "How are we going to do that? The mad scientists will turn into a ravening demon if we undo these bonds."

Mayumi giggled again, getting into the spirit of the thing, though the old radio show and comic references were completely obscure to her. She immitated a terrifying roar to the best of her ability, and struggled futilely with the hose that bound her to the bed. They undid her belt and pulled her dress up to her shoulders. Her pantyhose followed, and they were left with the problem of getting them over her feet and the bonds.

"Got a problem?" Mayumi asked maliciously.

"No!" they both said after a moment of study. Jim immediately started tickling her with one hand while holding her leg with the other. She giggled and struggled, trying to kick as Andy quickly slipped off the restraining loop, pulled off her skirt and one leg of the stockings. The action was repeated with the other leg. The arms soon followed. She was naked, spread on the bed now dressed in nothing more than a small gold chain around her neck.

The patch of fur at the base of her belly was small and elongated, framing the tiny pink lips delicately. Jim opened the stopcock on the vial carefully. A single drop of pink fluid emerged from the bottle and dropped onto the soft pussy mound. The bottle was laid aside and the two men bent over to feel the effects of the perfume. It had been compounded largely of natural fragrances, and Jim thought he could detect sandalwood and the faint touch of sweet olive among other things. His fingers and Andy's meshed as they rubbed the drop thoroughly into her pussy, tracing the length of her lower lips with their fingers, dipping lightly into her already moist cunt. Jim found that his pants were constricting him. Andy, Mayumi could see, was already under the influence of the pheromone. His half-erection had now turned in a full tumescence and the length of his shaft was banging against his belly. Jim started to strip hurriedly, then slowed down when he saw from Mayumi's eyes that she enjoyed the performance. Soon however the effects of the sex pheromone in the perfume were in evidence. All three of them were panting heavily and Mayumi's struggles against her bonds were the struggle of desire for physical contact.

Andy poised between her legs and her eyelids almost closed in anticipation. He held down the tip of his cock with an effort, aimed at her wet opening, then pushed forward. They cried out in unison and Jim was hard put to maintain his patience. She turned her head blindly aside as Andy started moving in her channel, and Jim took that as an invitation kneeling by her head and presenting his aroused cock. She sucked the male pillar into her mouth, still moaning as she began sucking helplessly at the male flesh. Their joint first orgasm was quick and sudden. They all clutched one another hungrily, then relaxed their holds. The men changed places. Andy's cock tasted of the mixture of his and her juices, and Mayumi swallowed hungrily. Jim's cock was a slick solid presence between her legs. All three of them moved together slowly and dreamily at first, reaching for the next eruption. TO HERE

Later, almost satiated, she examined the huge bathroom with appreciation. It was the sort normally seen only in inns. The bath itself was large enough to hold several people in complete comfort, it was stepped so that a reasonable bath could be provided for a smaller number. The water was fed in through a stone waterfall. One side of the bathroom consisted of a single large window which looked out into a tiny walled garden. The floor of the bathroom was covered by cedar wood slats which smelled gently of forest and fresh air, an impressions strengthened by the ferns and half-hidden aquarium fish besides the waterfall.

"This was the reason we took the house," Jim said proudly.

"Yes, I know it. Kitamura *sacho* bought it some years ago." She laughed at his expression, then linked her arms with those of the two men. "He thought you'd be insulted if he told you he had bought it for you."

They soaped her thoroughly and were soaped in return, then sank gratefully into the hot water. The window was open and the late evening sounds of Tokyo were barely audible. The smell of sweet olive penetrated through the window and Mayumi could see the tree's tiny pink-orange blossoms from where she sat in the water, cradling two feet, one Andy's, one Jim's in her lap. They talked about their work and their interests, and she rubbed the men's toes into the warm folds between her legs, smiling mischievously.

"I'm thirsty," Andy said. he rose to his feet in the bath and climbed out. Mayumi watched his behind appreciatively, then found her attention being distracted by Jim's foot whose big toe was worming its way into her sensitive cleft.

Wearing two bottles of Sapporo Lowenbrau beer, three glasses, a tray and a smile Andy was caught unaware by the two silent visitors in the entrance way. They looked at his nude form with fishlike expressionless eyes. Their crewcuts and black suits gave some hint to their identity. Nervously, but ever so carefully Andy lowered the tray.

"Midlaa-san?" One of them said in a deceptively gentle voice.

Andy gulped, wished Sissy McLane, the only friend he had with any combat experience were there, and wished himself elsewhere simultaneously. He said nothing.

"You have a package here. We wish to buy it," the man continued. There was still no expression on his face, and no word nor movement from his companion.

Andy took a nervous step backwards. Dealing with *yakuza* types was not his forte. His rump bumped against some furniture. He softly put the tray down and reached behind him. Holding the telephone of its hook gave him a bit more confidence.

"I don't know what you are talking about," he said in honest puzzlement.

"Kitamura Dansuke? He sent you a package. We want it."

"Its gone," he said.

The second *yakuza* started to move forward, and was restrained simultaneously by his companion and by the weapon in Andy's hand. "All I have to do is push one more number," he said in a quiet voice. "The police box is only around the corner."

"We are ready to negotiate," the man said, still not moving. "One million yen."

Andy shook his head silently. His throat was dry. "Go," he mouthed silently. The two hoods looked for one long, terrifying moment at Andy, then slipped out the door and were gone. Andy slumped against the antique *tansu* he and Jim had bought. His body was covered by gooseflesh. He was grateful they are gone. He was no hero himself, and the thought of what they could have done to himself or to Mayumi or Jim was terrifying. He decided not to mention it to her. Safer that way until she delivered the package. And that had better be done soon. He composed himself, took a long swallow of beer, and whistling to the best of his ability returned to the bathroom.

"There's something funny going on, isn't there?" Jim asked the following morning. Andy had insisted on placing Mayumi into a cab himself, even going so far as to instruct the driver and pay him in advance. He had been nervous and preoccupied the previous night, and to Jim's frustration, Mayumi had said she was feeling the heat and was not interested in love.

"There is indeed," Andy said morosely. He told his twin of the previous night's visit.

"Shit, you fucker. Don't you realize you've put her in more danger?"

"Why? She's going straight to the company offices . . ."

"You're an idiot," Jim stormed. "They could have taken her any time."

"In Tokyo? From a taxi? You know even the *yakuza* couldn't do a thing like that."

Jim was slightly mollified. Tokyo has the highest ratio of policemen to citizens of any megalopolis in the world, and the lowest rate of violent crime.

His unease was justified when the telephone rang.

Andy put the telephone down gently. He stared wide eyed at Jim. His brother looked back anxiously.

"Boy, are we in trouble! Mayumi did not make her

appointment. She's disappeared. And Dads seem to think we had something to do with it."

"There's something just as bad," Jim reported white faced. Something had occurred to him, and he had disappeared in the direction of his study just as the phone rang. "She took the tape with her!"

They looked at one another in growing consternation.

CHAPTER 9

ENTER THE FLAGON

The handsome man in the bed turned to look thoughtfully at his companion. She was still breathing heavily, and her breasts rose and fell with her breathing. He squeezed one of her mounds, and she groaned in appreciation.

"I don't think I can do it again so soon, honey," she said in a pronounced American accent. "this is the first time I've ever had enough."

He chuckled coldly. "Then I'll just enjoy myself, if you don't mind."

The silk sheet rustled as he swung over her chest. She divined his intention easily and squeezed her breasts together. He slid his long thin cock between the two warm soft mounds and began fucking her tits. His movements were first slow, then they speeded up as her sweat and the preliminary discharge from his cock moistened her skin.

"Leon, I have to talk to you!"

He twisted his neck to seek the source of the voice. "Not now Ruby. I'm busy."

"Now!" the dark young woman commanded.

"Who is this?" The woman beneath Leon shrieked.

"Only my interfering cousin. Ignore her, Love." He shoved himself briskly between her tits once more, and when she was inclined to argue, pulled at her head and inserted the tip of his cock into her mouth. She sucked at it avidly. Notwithstanding her embarrassment she was curious about this view of the private doings of the Typhon family.

"Very well," Ruby said, seating herself on the side of the bed. "Later."

She contemplated the splayed pale body on the black sheets. "I'll help you." She slipped a strong square hand between the woman's spread legs. Blunt expert fingers searched the moist crannies of the woman's cunt and stroked the clitoris expertly. The woman receiving Leon's cock in her mouth arched her body with pleasure and responded with growing cries to the invasion of her body. The rush of Leon's semen into her mouth choked her and dribbles of white gluey fluid ran out of the corners of her mouth. He stabbed as deeply as he could, squeezing her breasts together painfully while he emptied himself. At the same time Ruby's skillful fingers brought the woman on the bed to a climax of her own and her thighs clamped over their searching digits, covering them with rich essence.

"Well? Want to justify this?" Leon said as his bed companion retired to the adjoining bathroom.

"Aunt Mary." Ruby said.

"Who is Aunt Mary?" Leon said raising his eyebrows.

"Don't play games with me, Flagon. I'm much smarter than you."

"You really think so?" He asked with raised eyebrows, though her use of his commercial code name was a thrust he could not ignore. "Well, anyway, she is dead. Even I barely remember her."

"I said stop playing games. I'm talking about her offspring . . ."

"Which one?" he asked lazily. Then his jaws snapped shut. He had not realized she did not know there were two of them. He shrugged mentally. The cat was out of the bag now.

"This one," she said, shoving a picture beneath his nose. It showed a serious young man wearing sunglasses in an oriental setting. "Who is he?"

"I couldn't tell, dear cousin," he said grimly. "They're twins you see. Unusual too, as is everything our family produces. Single egg, fraternally different. And they haven't been raised as Typhons."

""Explain that," she said. There was some doubt in her voice.

"Our dear aunt had two men in one night. She was fertile that night apparently and had her single egg fertilized by two sperms."

"Impossible," Ruby snorted.

"Highly improbable," her cousin agreed. "But impossible? That word cannot be applied to a Typhon."

She smiled, then her expression hardened. "Why are you attacking them then?"

"They're Typhons only by accident," he said. "Besides, I have nothing against them except that they are the key to their fathers, and sometimes a hindrance to me. I've been trying to get something from those old farts in Japan for more than a year now. They have a new line of scents which is most promising. They have been gradually taking away our business, these Nips, in a number of ways. Now the rumor has it that they have developed a new scent, or process, which just might blow our investments out of the water. I'll not permit that. I have tried to reach them through the two young bastards, but so far have had no luck. My agents failed me twice already, and I've just given the lot of them hell over the phone. They can barelyu speak any English but I made myself perfectly clear. I'll have to go to Japan myself."

"Why? Do you think they'll wilt away at the power of your name? We have not had any business in Japan directly, and from what I gather, doing business there is not at all easy."

"My kind of doing business is always easy. They're as greedy as anyone else, and as subject to pressure. I also have a contact there, in Yokohama. I'm told social ties are important, and I have a membership in a club with a branch there. That and Typhon *elan* is all I need."

"I've never liked the cold-blooded way you do business, Leon. I think there's something more to it. I don't want those two young men hurt. Besides the fact that they are cousins; which makes them family by *my* book, even if not by yours, *I* think they're good looking. At least the one in the picture is, and if they're identical as you say. . . ."

His voice hardened. "Hire them as concubines then, if you've taken a fancy to them. But *I* need them first. I'm in charge of fashion and perfumery, and they are part of my plan for access to the Clouds and Rain corporation. You have no idea what is involved, and I won't tell you either. You can go to the board and have me dismissed if you think you can do it. Otherwise stick to your engineering and construction business."

His grin infuriated her. He was right, according to the rules by which they both lived. The Typhon family was large, extremely wealthy, and had manifold business interests. Younger members gradually acquired power and responsibility as they entered the family business, and Leon, as everyone recognized, was the rising star of the younger generation. She supposed that at some stage she would have to have a child by him: the Typhon clan were firm believers in breeding their way to success, and encouraged their younger people to experiment and to produce offspring. Extraordinary ones like herself and Leon rose in the family councils, the unintelligent and dull were pensioned off to Cannes or Paris where they unwittingly maintained the Typhon cover as a rich but unambitious family. She sighed internally. There was really nothing more to be gained here. She rose and stormed out of his bedroom.

Leon watched her go. It was not like Ruby, brightest among his cousins, to act as if she were an impulsive female. In some ways, he was ready to acknowledge, she was his superior. Power putches were a fact of life inside the clan, but he and Ruby had never clashed before. The Typhons were more a clan held together by mutual support and interest than an extended family, and he wold like to have kept Ruby on his side. But the Japanese matter was urgent: urgent for the Typhons and urgent for his own personal success.

Narita airport was like any other Leon had seen. His hired limousine, the driver puckishly wearing white cloth gloves, was waiting as expected. He wondered whether to approach his cousins directly. He did not think of Jim and Andy as such in his mind, but recognized the blood, if not the family connection. On the other hand, he needed to find some dependable agents first. And in such a case, it would be best to establish himself and familiarize himself with the city first.

Sunk into his own thoughts he did not notice another limousine following his own on the sixty-kilometer ride to Tokyo. Ruby grinned in satisfaction through the window. Leon's weak point was his utter disregard for others, and his contempt for their abilities. She had watched him comfortably on the long flight from Amsterdam from behind a blonde wig, dark glasses, and heavy makeup. She was amused to see him set his eyes on one of the First Class stewardesses. First class was uncrowded and she had watched with delight, her hand between her legs, as Leon and the stewardess had made silent furtive love in the galley. It was only with great effort that she managed to restrain herself from pinching the stewardesses delightfully smooth pink buttocks as Leon's long prick shuttled back and forth into her sighing and moaning form.

Now here they were in Tokyo, she for the first time, and he was still unconscious of her presence. She wondered if the same could be said for the two mysterious cousins she was hoping to meet.

CHAPTER 10

TRAVEL TAX

"The first thing to do is find where she has gone," Jim said. They were operating on borrowed time now. They were not sure Kitamura and Fine would retaliate, but surely they would do something, if only out of loyalty to an employee.

"How?" Andy asked practically. "We're not policemen, and I for one have no idea how to go about it."

"Ah," Jim said raising and admonitory finger. "But we do know some police. Women that is."

"Brother mine, now I know why I keep you around."

Finding Michiko Teraoka was no problem. She was part of the neighborhood police force. She had no knowledge of any kidnappings or accidents to anyone answering Mayumi's description, and promised a more thorough search. She was obviously curious, but was able to restrain her professional inquisitiveness upon promise of full disclosure. Later. In private.

"Now Sissy," Andy prompted.

"I hope she's still there. Last I heard she was supposed to be reassigned, remember."

Andy shrugged. "No harm in trying." He grinned reminiscently. "Promise her what you promised Michiko. We haven't had her black ass for ages."

"Don't you think of anything but your cock?" Jim asked. "This is serious!"

"True, but what has that to do with the price of tail?"

To their surprise and relief Captain C.C. McLane, US Army Counterintelligence was in, and more than delighted to talk to an old lover or two.

"Jim boy, can I get you to sign up again? Want to get back in uniform?" Her deep throaty chuckle was infectious, and the double entendre obvious only to the three of them.

"I'm still sore from the last time," Jim confessed, laughing in turn. His voice became serious. "We need some help, Sissy."

"Again? What sort of trouble you boys in this time?"

"Real trouble, I'm afraid. We're spreading a net. A friend of ours has disappeared and we want your help in finding her."

"Mr. Suzuki, what gives you the idea I'm here as a lost and found department for your girlfriends?" There was a hint of frost in her voice.

"No Sissy," Jim protested. "This is serious. She's my dads' assistant, and she was carrying something terribly important. We think she might have been waylaid."

"What an old-fashioned word," Sissy said musingly. "I'll try to help. She American?"

"No. Japanese. But I imagine your sources are better than ours." He have her the information she needed, and in return, suggested she look them up.

"Once I'm over jet-lag my boy. I've just gotten back from Germany. And you two better watch out, cause I've got a powerful hunger in me."

"We'll be there." Jim promised

"Here? At the base?" she asked in surprise.

"No, there, in you," he chuckled, and having the last word, hung up.

The day was nerve wracking for both young men. They paced the new house nervously, snarling at one another.

It was late in the afternoon when Sissy called. A girl

answering Mayumi's description had boarded a flight to the US the previous morning. The flight had been booked by an agent in Harajuku, a trendy area of Tokyo. The girl had appeared worried and frightened.

Michiko called later. There was information on the streets of a deal between one of the Tokyo *yakuza* families and someone overseas regarding a new drug. The *yakuza* source said that the drug came from a young woman whom they had contacted the previous day, though the information about it had originated overseas.

Jim and Andy looked at one another in dismay. Things were getting to be very hairy if the Japanese underworld was seriously involved.

"You thinking what I'm thinking?"

"Yeah, that we better tread real carefully here."

"Lets find out where she went. . . ."

"Travel agent. Maybe we can get some information out of him. And perhaps Michiko Teraoka's source?"

"You ready to mess with the *yakuza*?"

Andy looked out the window, shuddering. Neither he nor Jim were in any way capable of violence, at least not the sort of violence where anyone could get hurt seriously. And the previous day's encounter still sent shivers down his spine, even though nothing had happened. "We don't have much of a choice, do we? For all Dads' regard for us, I have the idea they are tough cookies. And anyway, we owe Mayumi. I just wish we had Sissy here to bodyguard us."

"The travel agent it is. I hope he's amenable to a little bribe."

In the event he wasn't. Or rather, he was a she. The two brothers went into a well-rehearsed routine, one that had worked before in other circumstances. Ten minutes after they had entered the cramped little office they were talking amiably with the operator, a short woman with a remarkably large bust and a smooth heavily made-up face. She professed amazement that two foreigners were interested in her operation, and was no less surprised at Andy's analysis of her cash flow problems.

Jim was leaning over her desk rapidly demonstrating an improved ticketing sub-procedure on her computer terminal while Andy was regaling her with a scheme to manipulate currencies. Business did not appear to be brisk. The heat was keeping people indoors, and her tiny office had no air conditioning. Unconscionsly she undid the top button on her blouse and moved uncomfortably. Andy finished his presentation, and rose to examine the poster covered wall of the office. he stopped before a poster advertising the cool delights of a New Zealand mountain resort. Two skimpily clad Japanese models were sunning themselves by the stream.

''Isn't one of these lovely lady's yourself, Ando-san?'' he asked mischievously, turning as he did so.

Her head turned to him in a flash, and he saw her hand withdraw from Jim's leg. She was sitting on a swivel chair, and the rapid movement dislodged her, spinning the chair around and tossing her to the floor. She clutched at air and came up with the slack of Jim's pants. The jerk of the fabric pulled Jim out of whatever reverie he had been engaged in, as his pants slipped to the floor. He grabbed at his pants, overbalanced, and fell heavily onto her soft form. Andy rushed to their aid, tripped on the wastebasket and flopped forward, his face between her sprawled plump legs. He received a full whiff of her heated crotch as he struggled away, then saw she was not moving. Jim rose to all fours, peering into her face. Ando-san's face was red and she was struggling for breath.

''What the hell!!!'' they said in unison, then ''Water! No, artificial respiration!''

''She can't breath!'' Jim argued practically. ''Undo her shirt while I give her respiration.'' He bent to his task as Andy loosened the top buttons of her blouse and the zipper of her skirt. Beneath it she wore a brassiere and a slip. Both were tight and her full flesh bulged over the fabric restraints. Helplessly he appealed to Jim "What now? I can't undress her!"

"She's. Choking. Its. The. Heat." Jim said between puffs into the woman's mouth. "Open it!"

Andy hastily fumbled under her clothes and found the catches to her bra and slip. Soon her breathing eased and Jim pulled back. Her hands came up and clutched at his back. Her tongue darted into his mouth and her soft full lips sucked at his own. Then her eyes opened and she peered into his face. For a moment she debated whether to scream, apologize, or simply rise, and then, the decision made, she simply pulled his face to hers again.

Crouched over her, Andy detected the change in the tenor of the operation. mentally he shrugged, rose to his feet and headed for the door.

"Don't go," she whispered at Jim's ear. Andy looked back, his eyes on her. She was looking at him, fumbling with Jim's clothes with one hand, her legs still sprawled apart. he continued the motion he had started and the door locked with a click. Then he turned to her.

"Its too hot in here," he said. Her mouth was occupied by Jim's, but her eyes were on Andy as he performed a leisurely strip for her benefit. His shirt came first, exposing a smooth strong torso. His slacks followed and she admired his long muscular legs, so different from the bandy legs of Japanese men she had known. Finally, the black briefs followed as Andy pulled them down slowly over his hips, exposing a proud erection that filled up even as she watched.

He walked confidently towards her and knelt at her side on the dusty carpeted floor. She spread her legs to accommodate him, half afraid he would turn down her obvious offer. To her gratification she found his tongue laving at her heavy belly and his fingers parting the full lips of her femininity. She had a full, thick clitoris which peeped unabashed out from under the hood of her inner lips. Andy seized on the little cheeky nubbin with his lips and sucked at her energetically. With one hand she held on to Jim's head, forcing her tongue into his mouth then sucking his into her own oral cavity. At the same time she forced the other young man's head to her parted legs, moving about to direct his attention to the surfaces of her cunt. Andy slipped his tongue through the forest of black hairs that obscured her plump pussy lips, then slid it down the length of the inviting slit. Her hips heaved at him and only the pressure of her hand on the back of his head kept his mouth in place. He pushed both his hands under her, raising and pinching her full soft buttocks as he did so. She groaned in relief and released a flood of salty juices over his tongue. His finger joined his tongue at the entrance to her vagina, and while he worked his tongue back and forth, lashing her prominent bud, his finger penetrated her hungry hole, bringing down a fresh flood of inner juices. Her legs thumped unceasingly against the carpet until Jim feared she would bring someone up to investigate, then with a cry that echoed into his mouth, she gave a final convulsive heave and opened her eyes.

"That was wonderful," she said. Her eyes shon with heartfelt gratitude.

"Its not over yet," Jim warned her playfully. Andy made way for him and Jim slid down to take his brother's place. Andy contented himself with watching, occasionally squeezing or laving her breasts with his mouth while Jim brought the middle-aged travel agent to a conclusive climax.

They panted together in a pile, sweat beading their forms. Ando raised herself from the floor, vainly trying to dust her clothes off.

"I want to thank you boys," she said shyly.

They laughed it off, but it soon appeared that her gratitude was going to take a concrete and very delightful form. She had one of the widest and most mobile gapes Jim or Andy had ever seen. She knelt before them and pulled their erect poles towards her face. They inched forward and she inserted both knobs together into her warm mouth, then began to suck on them simultaneously. Both men looked on with amazement. Neither had ever seen nor experienced anything of the sort before. Using her hands she masturbated both shafts briskly and lovingly until both men thought they could stand it any longer. Their eruptions filled her mouth with their cream and they both trembled on their feet. She rose from the floor adjusting her clothing. A white sticky driblet led down from her lips and she licked it up unselfconsciously.

"Where did you learn to do that?" Jim marvelled absently.

She chuckled. "Tour guides have to learn many skills to be really successful."

They wondered under what circumstances she had applied *that* particular skill. They dressed, Jim hurriedly, Andy with more reluctance. He would have liked to stay and explore the possibilities in this relationship with the agent. She smiled at them cheerily as they left.

"Why did you want to leave so soon. We still don't have Mayumi's whereabouts."

Jim laughed. "Of course we do. What do you think I was doing with her computer? I called up all her seatings for the past twenty four hours. Mayumi left for the US on a flight last night. I would have ordered tickets from Ando-san but we still haven't had any confirmation from Michiko yet, and I wanted to be certain before we do anything."

There was a message on their answering machine from Michiko Teraoka. The source for the information she had originally supplied them with had been a woman, Uchida by name. She ran a small bar near Nakano station on the Chuo train line. Michiko had gotten the name from a detective friend by the name of Uchidah who had said that within limits, they could use his name.

The bar was one of the thousands that dot Tokyo. It was presided over by a thin intense woman, still showing signs of former beauty. Her hair was dyed a harsh red and her thing fingers were heavily beringed.

"Ah! a *gaijin*!" she said in loud surprise as Andy and

Jim walked in the door. The three customers at the bar raised their head perfunctorily then returned to their own business: bottles of beer and sake showed that they had been at it for some time.

They sat at the counter and ordered beer. She brought the Kirin and poured for them, lingering as if waiting for them to start a conversation.

"Hot today, isn't it?" Jim said after an appreciative sip at his beer. "You're Kurogi-san?"

"Of course I am," she swaggered somewhat. "Even *gaijin* have heard of me eh?"

"Yes. Uchidah-san told us all about you."

She peered somewhat nervously around, then laughed shortly "And how is the fat little sot?"

"I don't think he's as fat as you say," Andy said judiciously. "Nor as drunk as he pretends." He had no idea what Uchidah looked like, but from what he had seen of Japanese cops, "fat" and "sot" did not usually apply to them.

"Just testing," Kurogi said nervously.

Jim grinned. "We want to talk to you in private. About a friend."

She licked her lips, then walked over to the other end of the bar, clearing away bottles as she did so and replenishing little plates of pickles.

"I close in an hour," she said, still nervously.

"We'll wait. What've you got to eat?"

"Nothing for *gaijin*," she muttered.

"Try me," Andy grinned.

She smiled evilly, then placed a small dish with brown bits floating in a purplish-brown sauce before him. The little brown pieces were shaped like slices of soft rubbery celery stalk.

"Ah, sea cucumber," Andy exclaimed with relish. "Haven't had any in some time." He gobbled the lot happily while Jim looked on, somewhat horrified at his brother's obvious fondness for the more peculiar Japanese foods. He contented himself with *tofu* and fish flakes. The bar owner looked on with some amazement. Gaijin were notorious for being squeamish about the most tasty and innocuous dishes. On the other hand, they all stank of butter, or at least so she'd heard.

The last drinker staggered into the night. Kurogi-san switched off the outside red lantern and pulled down the indigo *noren* hanging that indicated, when hung, that her bar was open. She closed the door then wearily started stacking chairs.

The two brothers moved to help. She waved them away, but was obviously pleased by the attention. She addressed herself to washing the dishes and glasses.

''So what did you want?'' She asked over her shoulder.

''You told Uchida-san that you had some information. About a . . . substance. And a young girl who was carrying it.''

Kurogi spun around, her permed and dyed curls flying. She cast a quick glance at the door. Reassured that it was still closed, she backed away from them. ''Are you mad? You know what would happen to me if it became known that I give information?''

''Its for a friend. We must rescue her,'' Jim stared steadily back at her. ''You know the *yakuza* have a reputation for not harming the innocent, would you like the tradition to be broken? She is not involved in drugs. It must have been some sort of mistake.''

''Why should I help another woman?'' she asked. Some of the brass had returned to her voice.

Andy leaned over the bar and looked back earnestly. ''Surely you can't want an innocent girl to come to harm? And we love her very much.''

''Both of you?'' There was a hint of incredulous laughter in her voice.

''Yes, both of us. She was visiting us and was supposed to be somewhere the following morning. Today that is. No one has seen her since. We are extremely worried.''

''She spent the night at your place?''

They nodded in unison.

''Which one did she sleep with?'' she asked curiously. ''Who is her lover?''

''Me,'' each of them said.

''Both of you eh? What a woman. I'm sorry I spilled her beans.''

''No, I mean . . . well, there were no beans to spill.'' Andy had noticed the voyeuristic gleam in Kurogi's eyes. ''She slept with both of us.''

''Very cozy,'' she commented.

''Yes, it was,'' Jim said, seeing where the conversation was heading and hoping to use it as leverage. ''I have a large double *futon*, you see.''

She giggled at the impropriety. 'Double *futon*' implied sexual activity, and it was not a term used in polite company. ''You mean together?'' The scandalized tone in her voice was faked, but the delight in uncovering such behavior was quite genuine.''

''Yes,'' Andy said coming around the bar and touching her arm. ''Surely you've tried that? I mean a good woman can easily tire out two men . . .'' he stroked her forearm mutely.

''You *gaijin*!'' she exclaimed in delicious shock. ''Such ideas! Akebono, my steady would kill me for even thinking about it.'' And yet the thoughtful look on her face was saying something else.

''You mean you've never tried that?'' Jim pursued, while maneuvering himself to her other side. His thigh brushed hers and he fancied he could feel a slight tremor.

''It's disgusting!'' she said loudly.

''Why?'' Jim asked. His voice was down to a purr and his hand rested quite frankly on her curving belly. On her other side Andy was stroking her forearm and leading her hand slowly towards her crotch. Jim found the light switch and dimmed the bar lights as his hand slipped into the waistband of her skirt.

She slumped against the serving area as their experienced hands made shoprt work of her objections. Jim's hand's crept higher until the palm of his hand was rubbing slow circles across her tight sweater. The nipple promptly sprung erect and pointed back at his hands. He squeezed gently while leaning over and blowing into her ear. Kurogi shivered and Andy tok the opportunity to dip into her waistband. She sucked in her belly to allow him access and the tips of his fingers scratched at the top of her flattened bush. He bent his knees and raised her calf-length dress, sliding his palm the ength of her thigh. Nylon whispered beneath his hands and he stroked the muscular leg without a word. The only sound was the whispering of fabric and her own breathing. Her hands clenched and the long painted nails dug into her palms. She knew she had lost, and te idea of having two men appealed to her enormously. She had had men serially, but never together, and these two were obviously willing. In the meantime, she surrendered to the sensation.

Jim was now nibbling at the side of her neck. Kurogi's head fell forward, and he nibbled his way to her nape. She shivered again, and spread her legs wider to allow Andy some access to her moistening pussy. he approached the target slowly, rubbing her thigh in slow sensuous circles. He pulled at her hose and exposed more of her belly. She turned to face him and Jim crowded up behind her. His hands were full on her breasts now, squeezing and tickling the nipples. At the same time his tongue and breath were working wonders on the back of her neck. Kurogi moaned slightly, then felt her hand being held. A warm, thick object was placed in her palm and the *gaijin* before her pushed forward while pulling her nylons and panties down her thighs.

"No, not here," she groaned. "My room is above." She hurriedly let go of the two erections and led them, almost at a run, through a small door in the back of the bar, along a narrow corridor and up a creaking set of stairs. A dim light illuminated a simple room hung with glossy posters and calendars. Many of them displayed girls from a dance troupe, and a younger Kurogi looked out of them, singly or as member of a posed group. A single *futon* was laid in the center of the floor. The *tatami* mats were musty and old, but the bedding and sheets were crisp and clean. She had obviously prepared her bed earlier, before going down to work. She led both men deliberately towards the bedding.

''It is a bit narrow,'' she said. her voice was shy, now that they had finally arrived at the situation she lusted for, yet was afraid of.

''No matter,'' Jim soothed her, his lips nuzzling at her neck. Andy quickly bent and flipped the upper cover away. ''It is hot today. This will do service as a mattress as well.

They stripped her, using their mouths and hands on the exposed skin. She had run to fat, as athletes do, but under the looseness could still be felt a dancer's supple muscles and joints.

Jim took possession of her feet. Her ankles and calves were smooth and strong. He kissed the insides of her calves, gradually moving upward with little flicks from his tongue. The trail of his passage glistened in the dim yellow light of the night lamp. he reached her knees and the parted eagerly, offering him a full sight of her open cavern and the fringe of black hairs at the base of her belly. Her face and breasts were hidden by Andy's shoulders.

Andy tried to kiss her, but Kurogi turned her face away. Instead he nibbled at her ear and neck, gradually descending to her chest. Her nipples tingled in anticipation and her hands searched for his head. His hair was slightly curly, and far softer than any man's hair she had touched. She peered downwards just in time to see his lips engulph one of her nipples. She hoped they would do this for a long time: men mostly were too eager to insert themselves. She trembled slightly as the feel of both mouths reached a critical point. The other one was kissing the insides of her thigh now and she wondered when he would stop.

Andy shifted to the other rbeast, sucking as much of the soft femalness into his mouth as he could. His tongue did duty as finger, strumming the erect nipple. he bit it gently and was rewarded by her hand clamping into his scalp. He screwed hie eyes up at her in the dimness and smiled as well as she could. She was watching the activity, her eyes almost closed.

Suddenly her body stiffened. She squealed in surprise and Andy was almost thrown off her chest. Then her head tilted back and her mouth opened in a long moan. She had never felt a like sensation, though it had been described to her by girlfriends. She hoped it would go on forever, and the doubts she had still harboured about the two men vanished without a trace.

Jim continued licking and kissing his way up her thighs. He sniffed at the rich aroma between her legs, then delicately reached for her inner lips with his tongue. At first there was no reaction, then when he ran his mouth the length of her slit he was rewarded by a flurry of tremors in her skin, and by a sudden spasmodic bucking in her hips. Eagerly he set to work, kissing and laving the length of her cunt with all his might. His fingers spread the delicate lips and he sought for and found the button of her clitoris. Sharp nails dug into his scalp as she urged him on.

The ceiling finally returned to focus. The loud sound of breathing was her own, and the sensations in her cunt had not ended. No man had ever doen that to her before, and Kurogi could now understand why Akebono, her current lover, was so insistent on having her suck his pole. It was wonderful. But now that she had come with the man's mouth on her, she wanted more.

Jim pulled his mouth away from the woman's demanding soft cunt. His face was wet and he needed some air. Besides, his rod was as stiff as iron, and the time, as far as he was concerned had come. He raised her feet in the air and squatted before her. His hands guided the head of his erection to the sweet wet opening into her body. he moved the head about in the opening for a moment, savouring the wet hole that opened and seemed to try and gulp him, then leaned forward and shafted her depths with one smooth movement. Her channel contracted around the invader and Jim grasped her calves firmly as he set to work to fuck her.

Andy redoubled his efforts at her breasts as he felt her knees on his back. She was grunting, tiny feminine grunts of pleasure and effort as Jim pumped himself into her. The sound was complemented by the wet slap of Jim's thighs and balls against her own skin. Andy squeezed her flesh and was rewarded by her hand on his head. Her own head started thrashing from side to side on the futon, her red hair flying in gorgon locks. Andy slipped out from under her legs and watched his brother move. His own hand stole to his erection, and then he brought her long-nails in contact with her shaft. Eagerly she stroked and felt his genitals as the movement's of her hips speeded up. Then everything was forgotten but for the male over and in her. She clasped Jim hungrily to her, bucking and pulling at him like a woman demented. Jim felt his shaft flooded with a copious discharge which ran down his thighs, matting the hair. She squealed once, loudly, and her hips arched high then collpased. Her knees gripped his sides hard, then relaxed fractionally. She turned her head to look at him, then spread her legs and arms exhaustedly. She pushed at Jim weakly, and he slipped off to one side.

She pulled them to her side, nestling between the two mle bodies. She was not finished yet, but the day had been tiring. The two men looked at her expectantly.

"My others are nothing like this," she said dreamily. "Akebono, my steady is always so rushed. Mind you, his cock is better, but what I get I get for myself."

"I hope he's not due here?" Jim asked in mock anxiety.

"No," she smiled. "Otherwise we would not all be here. Akebono called on me this morning. He was all excited. He and a friend had been hired to do a bit of work. They did it, but the deal was with a *gaijin* from Europe. he had said he wanted something from this girl, see, but he hadn't said anything about drugs. She had this bottle with her with a special stopper. Obvious it was drugs, ne? So they took that, then called their employer. Had a terrible row. It turned out the man was interested in something else—a tape or something—which Akebono had let go with the girl. They had a fight on the phone. I can just imagine Akebono having a fight in English. Huh! So Akebono doesn't have the laboratory, But he decides he's going to manufacture this stuff himself. He's had some business in Thailand and in Pakistan, buying poppers. So he's heading there. That's all I know. The girl? She went off somewhere."

No questioning, subtle or otherwise could produce any more information. Kurogi simply did not know. Their questions dried up. Their hands started to stroke the length of her body once more. She found herself ready again, rested, alert. This time the paler one headed for the juncture of her legs. She felt for their poles. Akebono's cock was knobbly—a common *yakuza* practice since he had inserted small marbles into the skin—and these were smooth. Nontheless they were hard and erect and would do admirably. Andy's mouth was soon exciting her close to a climax again. Jim was nibbliong alternatively at her breasts and her ears. She wanted a change, and pushing him off she rolled Andy onto his back. He held his shaft up for her inspection. She straddled him and fed the length of the shaft deeply into her wet interior. She felt around the base with her fingers. Their hair were perfectly meshed and she could feel the balls sprouting from between her thighs. Kurogi started bouncing over the supine man, gradually increasing her tempo. The young man under her cupped her full muscular ass in his hands and helped add lift. Jim squeezed her breasts while nibbling away at her shoulders. She saw his prick. It was erect and firm as before, and she knew he had not come into her. A perverse desire invaded her. She reached for his cock and brought it to her mouthg as she bounced on the other. Jim stood up before her and as her mouth sucked rythmically at the top of his shaft and one of her hands clutched his hip, she rode Andy furiously and felt his balls at the same time.

Kurogi felt herself peak just as the first preliminary drops from Jim's cock spattered her tongue. She sucked at the fluid avidly, not wanting to miss any of the sensation. The man beneath her was also crying out loudly, his hands fondling the lips of her cunt which were distended around his maleness. Then she felt she forceful hosing of her insides which indicated he was coming. Her own hjuices gathered and moistened her internal channels still further. She jerked on the cock that impaled her, while at the same time sucking as well as she could at the other staff. For a long moment all three of them were still, only the trembling and pumping of their hips indicated life. A few drops escaped Kurogi's lips and trickled down her chin. The white pearls complemented those that beaded Andy's belly and pooled between their skins. Then all three of them rerlaxed and sank to a tangled heap on the crisp white bedding.

Dawn was tinging the sky and the trains had barely started running as they found themselves before Nakano station again.

"We've got to get both back again" Jim said.

"Yeah, how?"

"You'll have to deal with the vial of perfume, I'll follow the girl, since she has the tape, or at least, I hope she does."

"Thanks a lot bro. The vial goes with what is apparently a very nasty and confident *yakuza*."

"A Japanese *yakuza* and therefore out of his element," Jim reminded him.

Andy grunted. "I suppose so. Though if I don't come back, it'll be because someone stuck a knife between my ribs."

"Your stomach," Jim said absently.

"Huh?"

"Your stomach. The *yakuza* always knife people in the stomach."

"How do you know?" Andy asked suspiciously.

"Late night movies, how else?"

CHAPTER 11

PALM DAYS

Rice fields again, Andy mused as he looked down from the Thai Air flight as it made its final approach to Bangkok's airport. The fields were smaller, bordered by long bamboo-like plumes he assumed were coconut palms. The river valley was flat, dotted with tiny villages amongst whose house rose an occasional conical *wat*. Getting through customs was easier than in Narita: the Thais were obviously much more interested in visitors than the Japanese. The heat smote him as soon as he had left the plane, and the coolness of his air conditioned hotel room was a blessing. He had thought long and hard about how to find the slippery Akebono. Japanese tourists, particularly males, were all over Thailand. As were *yakuza* intent on their two major business interests outside Japan: importing female talent and drugs. He would have to tread very carefully here, if what he had heard about law enforcement in Thailand was true.

The thought of female talent brought an obvious solution to mind. He fished through his travel documents. The only persons he knew in Thailand were talents. Female. The Golden Girls to be exact, a rock band he and Jim had enjoyed some months before while searching for the Clouds and Rain Corporation in Gifu. He found what he had been looking for. It was his own card. On it, in a childish handwriting was written 'Krisha. Pattaya' and a telephone number. He sighed and turned to look for the map. When Krisha had left their hotel room that memorable evening, she had invited them to visit. But for all Andy knew it might have been just a gesture of momentary affection: easily performed and soon forgotten.

Andy picked up the phone and called the number. A male voice answered in sing-song Thai. "May I speak to Krisha please?" Andy asked in English.

"Who is speaking please?" the voice had obviously learned its English from an Englishman.

"My name is Andy Middler. I'm from Japan. I met Krisha and her group there, and I want to contact her."

"Is this a professional matter?"

"Excuse me, who are you?"

"This is her manager's office."

"No, I'm afraid not. Personal."

"Hm. Well I'm afraid she is not here in Pattaya. I will try to contact her for you. You are in Pattaya?"

Andy explained and closed the conversation by leaving his hotel phone number.

The phone rang an hour later, while Andy was debating whether to descend to the bright streets crowded with humanity.

She was not the only Thai woman waiting for an escort. Others, slim and beautiful, crowded the lobby. Jim rose to his feet from his seat in the hotel lobby, watching Krisha approach with admiration. In Japan, a prisoner of her contract, she was a thin, forlorn figure. In her own land, dressed comfortably for the heat in a neat batik dress and sandals, she fitted in to her environment. It showed in her carriage, in the way she greeted him, holding herself proudly before his admiring eyes.

"Andy-san? Is you?" Her Japanese was as poor as ever, but Andy fancied he heard real warmth in her voice. And, it appeared, she was anxious and willing to meet him. "I am glad you come." Her Japanese was no better, but even the language sounded better in her own land. he laughed with delight and took her small hand in his larger one. Her thumb was calloused from the guitar, but he was more conscious of the softness of her swaying thighs as she walked beside them.

"I need your help," he said, once their greetings had been performed. She listened wide-eyed to his explanation.

"Will cost money!" she warned seriously.

He smiled. He could afford it. "I'll hire you as my consultant. That way it will be a business expense, you get paid, I find the man I'm looking for, and the government pays because I'll put it down as a business expense."

She laughed happily. He hoped it was not solely at the thought of the fee. There were several phone calls to make, and visits to people and places in dark alleys and back-room offices he did not feel comfortable with. But soon the machinery of search was under way and Andy could relax and enjoy the sights.

Under her tutelage they explored Bangkok. She did not know most of the tourist haunts, taking him instead to her own Bangkok: the narrow waterways ploughed by slim-beamed praus, the floating market where he ate star-apples and chiclet fruit for the first time. Finally through the raucous streets set aside for entertainment.

They walked down one entertainment district. Slim girls in tight pants, short pants, short skirts, and probably little under them were walking through the streets. They were accompanied by men of all sizes, colors, shapes, ages, and presumably characters. Krisha laughed at Andy's open mouthed examination of the parade. Flashing neon lights declared "Fun!" "Dance" "Drink" and "Girls" Girls, girls.

"I buy you one?" Krisha said half in jest as they passed a shop front from which four young beauties in brief clothes gestured and smiled. There was only a tinge of jealousy in her voice.

"You are quite enough for me and much more beautiful," Andy said, squeezing her shoulders. She smiled back, perhaps not believing but content.

"I take you Thai bath. You like Japanese *ofuro*?" she asked suddenly.

"Always ready," he grinned and the colors of the fluorescents shon on his teeth.

They were ushered into a room decorated in bamboo and plastic greenery by two smiling hostesses. He and Krisha were stripped efficiently and impersonally and led to two raised massage tables. The bath, Jim discovered soon enough was the least of the service. Lying on his face he watched one of the silent masseuse rub Krisha lightly with a scented oil. Starting at the girl's neck the masseuse's hands made their way steadily and throughly down Krisha's back. he could feel the hands on his own skin, and the pleasures of sight and feeling reverberated against one another. The oiled hands descended lower down Krisha's back, then parted the slim small mounds at the base of her back. Krisha obligingly spread her legs and the oil-soaked hands dipped between her legs. She looked at Andy across the space that separated the massage tables. Her lips were open and moist, and her eyes half-closed with pleasure.

His own masseuse's hands had reached his buttocks. He parted his legs willingly and found her soft hand slicking the oil between his legs, then anointing the soft bag of his balls. he trembled slightly at the feel. The oil had been laced with some mild irritant, and he felt a growing fire in his loins. She motioned him to roll over and he presented her with the sight of a large erection. Without a change of expression she anointed his staff with the reddish oil. Krisha looked on curiously, aying something Thai which made all three girls laugh. Her own black delicate bush was being anointed and rubbed as well. She turned to look in Andy's direction. her mouth was working with pleasure and he could see that her nipples, coal black in the dim light, were hard and erect on her small brown breasts. He started to slide of the table, reaching for her, and she laughed gently.

"Not yet, Andy-san. You wait."

The masseuse's hand rubbed at his chest and belly muscles, lingering over his nipples, and then he was motioned silently on to his belly again. This time the two girls each produced a softened coconut husk. They began rubbing the rough fiber against the skin of his back. At first he found the sensation oddly uncomfortable, then as the dirt of the hot day loosened on his skin and the rubbing moved downwards, the brisk motions produced first a tingling, and then a burning fire in his skin that translated itself into a point in his loins. He looked at Krisha for guidance. The Thai girl had her eyes half closed and her hips were writhing as the brisk rubbing approached the crack of her ass. As she reached between Krisha's legs the masseuse started using a softer cloth, and Andy felt the same soft fabric being used gently against his balls, along the crack of his ass, and onto the length of his penis which was now jerking with impatient lust.

He truned over and the masseuse started on the muscles of his chest, working her way efficiently and thoroughly downwards. She reached his erect member and rubbed rubbed it to a shaft of fire. Andy rose suddenly. There was no way he could delay any longer. He had to bury himself in something before he burst. The masseuse slipped away from him and hurried to Krisha's side. Together they raised the supine girl's heels to her head, exposing her hungry, oil-glistening sex to his gaze. The swivelled her around so that her full stretched purse was open to his gaze, and then moved a lever to adjust the height of the table.

Andy took a step forward and one of the assistants hurried to his aid. She directed his rampant dick to the waiting smooth hole. Poising it at the entrance, she fed the shaft deeply into Krisha's hole. When the pubic hairs joined into a smoothly wet mass, she rapidly manipulated Krisha's tiny clitoris. Holding his ass lightly with one hand, she rubbed the base of his maleness in widening circles onto Krisha's crushed flower, then pulled back at the shaft, forcing Andy to withdraw. She pulled the cock completely out, and the other masseuse hurried to their side. She opened Krisha's delicate nether lips, showing the perfect pink inside as a delight for his gaze. Then his cock was led forward again. Sunk to the hilt he was manipulated again; pounding the mortar with his pestle.

They passed into a dreamy, effortless existence of pleasure. The entire act was controlled by others. He had no responsibility nor demands placed ion him save that he enjoy himself. When he got tired, a tall stool was slid under his buttocks. The two girls provided some oil which they spread beneath Krisha. Then they slid her body back and forth onto his erection, saving the two lovers the need for any effort.

Even his climax, when he came, was as powerful and as slow motion as anything in a dream. He rose from his stool and his masseuse clung to his back, using her weight to force himself deeply into Krisha. She reacted too, and her legs were held high, then brought over his back by the other girl who hugged Krisha's trembling and shaking form to his body.

Krisha opened her eyes and motioned him into the tub of warm water that dominated the far side of the room. The two girls promptly stripped, and as Krisha and Andy recovered in the tepid water, they coiled themselves around one another, rubbing themselves lazily, displaying one another's cunts, stroking their breasts, moving together in absolute sexual harmony.

Krisha noticed his growing erection, and called to them sharply. The two girls immediately assisted them in climbing from the bath. They were dried thoroughly in large towels. One girl knelt before Andy, the other before Krisha. Andy's semi-hard cock was sucked in by the girl's skilful lips. His erection rose readily and he started moving at her direction into her willing mouth. The other was servicing Krisha in the same way. Krisha said something, and they were led to a padded area of the bathroom. Andy was gently helped on to his back. Krisha squatted over him. The assistants crouched on either side of her slight form, then raised her in the air, dropping her in a complicated rhythm onto his erection. At another command from Krisha they released her and she sank deeply onto his cock. Lying on either side of the couple, the two girls raised one leg each into the air, exposing perfect, tiny fleshy flowers at the junctures of their thighs. They began masturbating, then Krisha led Andy's hands from her hips to the cunt on either side of his head. As he enjoyed the tactile and visual delights, her own hungry and skilled femininity milked him dry for the second time that night.

The streets were no less bright, still frenetic and active as they walked out of the bathhouse. Krisha nestled against Andy's satiated body.

"I work once as bath attendant. Good place, here. Not ripoff. This time first I am here as customer." She laid her head against his shoulder. "I stay with you tonight? Maybe later, you like some more?"

He squeezed her to him, which sufficed as an answer.

The phone rang at ten, as Andy tried in vain to cover his eyes against the morning's glare. Krisha reached for the phone and spoke high-pitched into it. The conversation took some time, and the only word Andy could understand was 'pakistan'. He hoped it did not mean what it sounded like.

"This Akebono you look for? He go Pakistan. Flight to Islamabad. Leave this morning six o'clock."

"With the vial. The bottle?"

"She say yes. She visit his hotel. You give some money for her information."

He surrendered the bhat, and cursed the Japanese for their efficiency and ability to rise early and go about their business. It would have been easy to arrange a small theft in Thailand. In Pakistan . . .

Krisha kissed him delightfully good bye, in front of the airport bus. She stood there, a slim figure in simple print dress waving gaily until the bus was out of sight on Bangkok's busy streets.

CHAPTER 12

KNIGHT IN PARADISE

Islamabad was cooler and drier than Bangkok had been, and Andy was grateful for the change. The city had been laid out in a new and ultra-modern a manner as possible, nd and yet it was already turning rapidly into the mental picture Andy held of a South Asian city. There were peddlers about. Women dressed in all-encompassing *chadours* rubbed shoulders with those in Western dress and were outline now against shanties, now against towering brick and steel and glass-modern monstrosities. Andy would have liked to see more of traditional Pakistan, but the need to find the phial was paramount. He knew little about the international drug trade, but if Krisha's information was correct, he would probably have to go to the center of it, near the Afghan border. The thought gave him the shivers: rude men in beards and turbans shooting at him was not his idea of a good time. There was one step he could take which might make reaching his objective easier: ask a native. On the other hand, the only native he knew could complicate his life enormously. He had debated with himself at length whether to call Amina. Finally he gave in. One look into the street convinced him that it would be impossible to do anything by himself, without some aid and information.

He called from the comfort of his air-conditioned room in the Royal Hotel. He knew hotel switchboards often listened in on their guests, and rather hoped they would: he had no desire to compromise Amina, who was now married, and he knew both of them would be circumspect with another ear to the phone.

A man answered the phone and said something in what Andy assumed was Urdu.

"Excuse me," he said politely. "My name is Andrew Middler. I am a former classmate of Amina Shah's. I happen to be in Islamabad and I wonder if I could speak to her?"

"A former classmate?" the man spoke excellent English with the musical, almost germanic pronunciation of most educated Indians and Pakistanis.

"Yes. From Japan."

"Ah! From Japan! This is her husband. I am afraid she is out. What was it you needed."

"Nothing really," Andy answered, his heart sinking. "I'm here on business. I wanted to say hello, and perhaps find out if she can direct me. This is my first time in Pakistan, you see."

"Business?" There was less suspicion in the man's voice this time, only a quickening of interest. "You do business in Japan?"

"Yes, I do," Andy said truthfully. Inspiration hit him. "Perhaps you are interested? Maybe we can meet? I mean, that would be better, talking to a colleague, you might say. I really am at a loss. I realize having been a schoolmate of Ms. Shah is not exactly a formal introduction, but I was hoping she would know someone interested in the Japanese market. . . ."

"Let me call you." There was much more cordiality in Amina's husband's voice now. "Where are you staying?"

Andy gave his hotel and room.

He collapsed on the bed, sweating heavily not withstanding the air conditioning. Cuckolded husbands in this part of the world, he remembered from his reading, tended to respond rather pointedly. Perhaps there would be no real need to meet Amina herself . . .

Shah called up thirty minutes later. "Mr. Middler? perhaps we could go to dinner, yes?"

"I would love that," Andy said truthfully.

"Do you know the Rajasthan restaurant? It is all the rage now. Perhaps we can meet there, yes? Ah, of course, you do not know Islamabad. The taxi driver will be able to tell you. . . ."

The Rajasthan was as opulent as it sounded. Ethnic dishes were apparently the rage. Shah turned out to be a mustachioed, thin, middle aged man with a large hooked nose and a closed expression. He wore a Western business suit, and Andy was glad he had dressed for the occasion. Amina sitting beside him, dressed in violet-red pantaloons and overshirt trimmed with gold was a complete contrast. Andy barely dared glance at her oval smooth face, noting nonetheless the movement of her breasts beneath the loose smooth fabric.

He shook hands with Shah as they sat around the low table, their shoes off. "Ogenki desu-ka, Shah-san?" he inquired of Amina, then continuing in English "Do you still practice Japanese?"

"Of course," she said, smiling charmingly. "I go to Japan several times a year. Have you been back?"

"Occasionally," he said.

That was almost the extent of their conversation, as Andy set himself to charm her husband. They ate an excellent *biryani*, complete with tiny dishes of various grilled and cooked muttons, flat breads, washed down with beer and flavored yoghurt.

Shah became voluble over the beer. "Wine of course is forbidden," he leered over his glass. "What we are drinking is of course is yoghurt." He pointed to the tiny drop of milky fluid on the saucer that had held his beer mug, and winked.

Andy laughed, and the laugh hid the flush that rose in his face at the memory of similar-looking drops of fluid on Amina's skin. She had come to his room to say farewell before leaving for Pakistan. They had been lovers for several months, and she had allowed, even encouraged Andy to make full use of her charms. Except for one thing. She had kept her vagina for the initial pleasure of her husband, and had sworn Andy to the preservation of her *virgo intacta*. Andy smiled into space and missed a few sentences of Shah's speech about the problems of doing business with the Japanese. he remembered instead Amina stretched out on the bed of his tiny one-room apartment. She had expressed a fondness for yoghurt, and he had been feeding it to her using the tip of his erect member as a spoon. The sight of her lying supine on his bed, her full ass rising before him, and the touch of her skillful tongue on the underside of his cock had brought him to a climax. With the final mouthful he had jammed the length of his cock deep into her throat and the yoghurt had mixed with the white spurts of his semen.

He returned to the presence and nodded mechanically at Shah's words. The conversation turned technical as they discussed import options into the Japanese market. Andy confessed himself interested in the pharmaceutical market. Shah looked at him sharply, smiled a small smile, and continued the conversation in a more thoughtful vein.

Amina watched the young European without seeming to do so. She was pleased Andy was carrying his side so well. The touch of his palm against her's as they had shaken hands brought back memories of the more recent past. She had run into Andy by accident. Shopping in Tokyo was one of her chief delights, and her husband could afford it. Later, with much trepidation she had visited Andy's apartment. She had had great pleasure with her husband, but she still felt she owed Andy something. Besides, she knew him to be a discreet lover, and it was time to find one. A rush of wetness caused her to squeezed her thighs together. Last year, for the first time, she had offered Andy her cunt. The thought of his ravaging maleness ripping through her tender tissues made the *lassi* she was drinking appear tasteless. She was conscious that her nipples had grown hard, and was grateful for the underclothes she had worn.

"By the way, is there a red phone here?" Andy asked casually during a break in Shah's monologue.

"A red telephone?" Shah asked in surprise.

"Of course," Amina said. "The public telephones are around that way."

She pointed to one side of the open sided niche they were dining in. Andy saw the minute flush of her face and knew she had understood him. He rose unhurriedly. "I have to make a call. Excuse me a moment."

He returned shaking his head. "The man will have an answer in fifteen minutes," he announced, resuming the conversation with Shah.

After his return Amina excused herself and headed for the toilets, while Andy and Shah began exploring the possibilities of cooperation. The Pakistan economy was stabilizing, and Shah was interested in opening the Japanese market.

The note from Amina was under the telephone. It was brief and unsigned. "Ten tomorrow."

The door to his room was unlocked the following morning and he was not surprised to hear it opening. The white, chadour covered figure was however startling. For a moment Andy did not move from the chair he was sitting in, then the woman, whoever she was, turned and locked the door, then turned back and chuckled softly.

Andy rose with a smile. "I see these things have their advantages," he advanced on her.

"Of course," she said. "Anonymity. No one would question my good intentions in a chadour. It also has some other advantages as well."

He knelt, then rose with the garment's hem in his fist. The rising hem uncovered her high-heeled shoes, then the length of black stockings reaching to the middle of her thighs. Above that there was nothing but soft warm brown skin to her waist. She giggled as his fingers slid cooly over her flesh. She had put on some weight since he had seen her last, but the addition only made her more alluring. He slipped the bulky garment above her head and stepped back to admire her.

"Now tell me, my knight, could any Western woman dress like this in public?"

Her mound had been shaven, exposing the length of her dark plump outer lips to his gaze. Around her hips she wore a thin gold chain. Her generous breasts were held up by an open gilt and enamel framework which exposed them completely. The nipples had been rouged, and her face had been carefully made up with deep kohl around the eyes and a bright red lipstick. Aside from these embellishments to her person, she wore no clothes under the enveloping *chadour*. She licked her lips, then swayed around showing her her rear. "Observe," she said. The thin gold chain around her waist dipped between the full moon of her ass. It was attached to a gilt dildo that had been inserted in her anus. Then she turned to face him again. "It is all yours, my knight."

Hypnotized by the sight, Andy stood still as she swayed towards him. Her shoulders, neck, hips and breasts all seemed to move independently. Gracefully she knelt before him. She unzipped his slacks and extracted his swelling shaft, then slid the crown into her mouth. For a long moment she merely sucked at it, moistening the tip with her tongue and palate, then vacuuming it with the movements of her cheeks and lips. Her eyes screwed up to meet his. Then she tilted her head, knelt further down towards the carpet, and like a python, swallowed the entire length of his cock.

Andy cried out in pleasure and surprise. She rubbed her large nose into the wiry hairs at the base of his maleness, then worked her mouth and throat simultaneously. His cock was caught in a muscular skilful vise. he could do nothing but stand there with his cock painfully yet pleasurably aimed down her throat. One of her hands was cupping his balls, massaging them tenderly, while the other was creeping into the crack of his ass. Then he felt her finger worm its way into his anus and stimulate the base of his penis.

He groaned again, almost a scream this time, and emptied himself furiously down her throat. She gulped and sucked, extracting the last of his juices, then withdrawing slowly from his shaft. The withdrawal was as exquisitely sensuous as the insertion, and he could feel the aftershocks of his own orgasm.

He collapsed backwards onto the bed, completely drained. Amina crawled up onto the covers, nestling her heavy smooth body against his side. Her heavy breasts lay partly on his chest and he squeezed them fondly.

"I wanted to give you pleasure as well," he complained.

"You have. You will," she said earnestly. "But you are my knight, my special one. It isa my pleasure to please you first. And you tasted so good. I delight in your flavor." She licked her lips again, like a satisfied cat.

"I'm rather surprised your husband let you come to the restaurant," Andy said. One of his hands was stroking her smooth cunt idly. It came into contact with the protrusion emerging from her behind and he wiggled it carefully. A shiver coursed through her body and she everted her buns against the pressure.

"My husband is very traditional," Amina said with a small laugh. "But since you are an old school chum, he decided on an exception. For one night only. He is interested in doing business with you. Is that really why you are here?"

Andy told her the story of the phial. She looked at him, troubled by his urgency. "Those are not good people," she said. "Even we, here in Islamabad are afraid of the Pathans. They control the drug trade out of Afghanistan, and this *yakuza* of yours is undoubtedly heading there. . . ."

"Is there any way of finding him, do you think?" He was practically desperate, and his worry showed plainly on his face.

She nodded. "I will help you, my knight. But you must

promise to be very careful. The Northwest areas are very violent, and many foreigners have disappeared there. Japanese are not all that common in the Northwest, however, and I have some friends who are the wives of prominent Northwesterners. It will take some time though.''

He squirmed around and pulled her hips to his mouth, then nipped the fleshy labia with his teeth ''So long as I am in this heaven, it cannot take too long for me.''

She laughed, pleased by the compliment and shoved her mound at his mouth. ''What would you like to do to me? What would you like me to do to you? I am all available. Take your pleasure my knight. Take me. Here, here are my breasts,'' She led his head to her breasts and he sank his teeth slightly into the prominent fat nipples. ''Ah, yes, again, so. Now. My belly, would you like to masturbate on my belly? Spurt you fluids onto my soft skin? My mouth perhaps? My back? Sometimes I lay flat on my stomach and he rubs himself fiercely against my back.'' With each word she changed position to allow him free access to herself. Now she turned and then bent over, exposing the crack between her mounds. The gold spike stood out, still tethered in place by the chain around her waist.

''What is this?'' he whispered entranced, touching the blunt end.

She laughed. ''I remembered our first encounters, and I decided to prepare myself if you wanted it. The spike keeps the muscles stretched and supple.''

Andy moved the shaft experimentally and she glanced over her shoulder. ''You can insert yourself into that hole too my love.''

''Would you enjoy that?'' he asked. His hands were almost trembling with anticipation.

''Of course,'' she whispered back. ''I will enjoy anything you do. The more you do, the more forceful you are, the better I will like it.'' She pinched her buttock hard, raising a mound of flesh.

Andy licked his lips again. "That could give you bruises," he said.

She chuckled. "That does not matter. He comes to me in the dark, usually, or fully clothed, as I am. Just so long as there is nothing to *feel*, it will be all right. Also, I have joined a . . . association. A Sufi society, and we sometimes strike ourselves in ecstasy. ." She rose and turned to face him and his hands went around her ample form.

"I am going to take full advantage of your beauty," he growled. His hands which had been stroking the full moon of her ass tensed suddenly and clutched handfuls of flesh. Amina's breathing quickened and she gasped at the pain but her eyes were full of delight and her lips caressed his neck.

"Slap me a couple of times," she said in excitement. "On my buttocks, on my breasts, on my mound!" Her eyes were rounded, huge and gleaming. Andy bore her down savagely, eager to please her and satisfy his own wildness.

He rolled her down on the bed, lust overcoming his judgement. He had prided himself before on his gentleness with women. Jim was occasionally the violent one, but here, with the opportunity virtually thrust at him, he was powerless to stop the upwelling of his own violence.

He slapped her quivering buttocks a few times. His blows were tentative, experimental in away. Amina, sprawled on his knees looked back reproachfully but said nothing. Driven by her glance, he smacked harder. She wiggled on his knee and he landed a flurry of blows against her behind.

She squealed, and the squeal, of fright and of joy, broke his last inhibitions. He rolled her onto the bed and struck earnestly at her quivering flesh. She rolled to get away. He seized one full breast and pulled her to him while smacking at the other quivering mound. Tears appeared in her eyes, but she was laughing as she lay there. Andy rose. His cock painful in erection. He slapped her full thighs apart and slammed himself down onto her body. His manhood penetrated her slit. She was wonderfully wet, her insides seizing onto his shaft like a baby reaching for a teat. He was cursing and crying as he rammed furiously into her. His hands clutched her buttocks, sinking into the velvety buttery depths. He encountered the chain, and for a moment did not know in his urgency what it was. Then he clutched hard at the metal, pulling it into her yielding flesh, forcing the cone deeper into her. She whimpered with pain, then laughed aloud as her own pleasure rose. *Now* he was acting like the knight of her dreams. Now he was on the road to real passion. The pain she felt was nothing compared to the pleasure of his insertion.

Suddenly he pulled away from her. She clutched at him in disappointment and he slapped her hand roughly away. He was scrabbling on the floor and she opened her eyes just as he rose, his belt dangling from his fist. His hair was disarrayed and there was a wild look she adored in his eyes. His hand rose and the belt swished down. It hit the inner flesh of her thigh and she cried aloud. Another blow and she whimpered, pulling her own reluctant thighs apart with her hands. The third blow landed fully on her shaven mound and she writhed in pain. he dropped the strap and was upon her muttering endearments as his lips soothed and cooled her hurt parts, his tongue dipping into her overflowing honey pot. Helplessly she jerked against that soothing mouth, again and again as her frame quivered with massive orgasm. He rose from her wildly again, and knowing his preferences, Amina trembled, then rolled over on her belly. She heard the swish of the strap again, and electric shivers ran through her body, along her spine, fleeing from the intensity of feeling as he hit her again and again, increasing the pleasure in her bruised pussy to a fever pitch. Then she was upon her again. His cock shafted mercilessly into the soft feminine center of her being. he fumbled at her backside. The golden cone was withdrawn suddenly from her bung. He stopped there for one second, slapped her quivering attentive flesh one time, then plunged the full length of his cock into her. At the last moment she contracted the muscles of her ass, making him fight his way into her.

The outpourings of his semen soothed the pain of his insertion in her flesh, and his orgasmic shaking and panting precisely matched Amina's own as they sank into the depths of a mutual orgasm.

CHAPTER 13

OF MICE, MEN, AND MUD

The ride from Islamabad to Peshawar was far from luxurious. Andy's mind was full of literary allusions, usually bloody, to the place of Peshawar in British colonial history. Peshawar itself was more ''oriental'' than Islamabad had been. Bearded Pathans roamed the streets, and small mongol-looking men sold carpets on every corner. The address supplied by Amina proved to be that of a high-walled villa on the outskirts of the town. Bare mountains rose higher towards the west and Andy knew he was at the entrance to the infamous Khyber pass. Less than a hundred miles from where he was standing, Afghan guerillas fought and died in the heat. The man he had come to see was a bald, wizened figure, snuffling to himself on a *charpoy* bed in a stuffy room. The silent servant who had let Andy in departed on noiseless feet.

As instructed, he handed the man an envelope. The old man counted the money carefully with snuff-stained fingers. Then he stared unblinking at Andy. He called out something, and another man, much younger entered the room. The two men examined one another carefully. The newcomer was dressed in loose pantaloons that had once been white. A loose shirt hung over the pantaloons. On his head he wore a woolen hat that seemed like an overly raised pancake. An ugly looking automatic rifle hung negligently from one hand. An uglier knife, its blade as long as his arm, was stuck into his belt.

"You come," he said.

"Hey, wait a minute, what . . . ."

The older man chattered something at high speed in a guttural language.

"You come. See Japan feringhee. He now make drug deal, but no one want buy. You come. See bottle."

Andy rose to his feet from the cushion he was on and followed reluctantly.

They walked through lanes bordered on either side by mud and galvanized iron huts. Andy realized that he was in a refugee camp. Large eyed children and chadour-covered women eyed him suspiciously. Occasionally a woman passed who was not covered. Several men dressed in little more than loincloths were working in a large pool of mud, making bricks. They mixed the slurry with their feet, then scooped the goo up into wooden forms. After several minutes the forms were tapped and a neat mud brick was added to the pile. Andy had never seen bricks being made before, and he watched curiously until they were out of sight.

The guide turned suddenly into one of the dilapidated houses. They slipped through several doorways, climbed a wall, then crept quietly into a house that appeared deserted. The guide motioned for silence. Finally they reached a tiny hole in the wall. The guide moved aside to let Andy see through.

A Japanese man in trim safari jacket was squatting in a circle with several bearded men. They were arguing hotly, but since the Japanese had to use an interpreter, the argument never reached the stage of violence.

"They say not drug. They say not laboratory make. Not possible."

"Yes, he's pretty mad too," Andy whispered back. "He says it only *says* perfume. In reality it is drug."

In truth, the *yakuza* appeared pretty desperate. It seemed

he had taken the bottle simply because his previous employer, whomever he was, had refused to pay. Now he was gloomily examining the bottle of SuccSex, not really knowing what to do with it.

"You go to Amsterdam. Amsterdam," the interpreter said loudly in heavily accented Japanese. Andy wondered where a Pathan in ragged clothes had learned to speak the language. "There is good laboratory. Maybe they help you." He muttered something to his companions in Pushtu.

Andy's guide grinned. "He say Japan man great fool. Taken in by woman's perfume."

"Can we get it away from him?" Andy asked.

The guide grinned in the dark. "No problem. You pay."

"I don't have sufficient money on me . . ." Andy had been warned by Amina not to admit to carrying cash.

"Two hundred dollar, you give."

"That's all I have," Andy muttered and forked over the money.

The Pathan guide's approach to theft was simplicity itself. Andy followed him through the labyrinth again, and they loitered in an alley waiting for the *yakuza* to appear.

The Japanese walked dejectedly out of his meeting. Two Pathan's were with him. Andy's guide casually raised his assault rifle, and before Andy could react, squeezed off a burst at the two guards and charged forwards. The guards fell, screaming horribly, and the large bearded young man, his gun still spitting death at the two, charged down on the small Japanese.

It must have been the first time he had ever faced anyone trained in karate, and the *yakuza* pride themselves on the quality of their training. The small Japanese screamed into action. A sickle kick moved the gun barrel aside, then his foot caught Andy's guide in the face. The *yakuza*'s hand darted beneath his jacket and emerged with an automatic pistol. It spat twice and the guide fell, a look of surprise on his face. Andy took one look at the carnage, then turned and ran. A swarm of men emerged into the alley behind him, fanning out quickly to avenge the murder of their brethren.

He skidded through alleys, climbing over piles of filth, looking for a place to hide, behind him he could hear the shouts of his pursuers. He would have to do something soon, or find himself impaled on one of those large knives, he thought numbly.

He passed a gate set into one of the mud walls. A young woman peered out of the gate. Her eyes widened at the sight of Andy's panting form. She stared at him in silence, then cocked her head to the sounds of shouting behind him. He stood there like a bull at bay, his sides heaving, pleading wordlessly. Wordlessly too she opened the gate and beckoned him. He tottered forward and into whatever sanctuary she had to offer.

The girl looked at the panicked westerner with amusement. Her regular, rather plain features were highlighted by a pair of magnificent green eyes. Large and luminous they transformed her face to one of elfine beauty. Andy looked at her with horror as he heard the rough steps approaching the compound. She cast a look at him, another at the gate to the compound, then beckoned him further in. Around the mud-walled shack she went. Beside a half-finished wall was a large puddle of deep-brown viscous mud. She made motions at him, muttering in some high-pitched language. He stared at her uncomprehendingly. It appeared she wanted him to undress. When he did not respond, stupefied by the request, she reached for him herself. He resisted for a moment, then after an obviously angry outburst from her, Andy stripped. She pulled impatiently at at his underclothes as well, sparing a long and admiring glance at his crotch before handing him two long strips of cloth. He peered at them uncomprehendingly, and she hurriedly wrapped one around his loins, the other around his head. Then she indicated he roll in the mud.

Dazed by now, Andy followed her lead. He rose from

the mud pool under her critical eye. Every inch of his skin was coated with mud. She smiled in satisfaction, then handed him a forme. This time he needed no instruction, hurriedly filling the forme he stacked half-dried bricks adding them to the pile besides the pool.

The three searchers stalked through the yard haughtily. Their guns were held in plain sight. The young woman harangued them shrilly, but they ignored her entirely. She screamed something at Andy when he paused from his work to eye the intruders, and he hurriedly obeyed her command to get back to work. The three Pathans sniffed at the half-naked *hubshi* taking orders from a woman, and left to bother the residents of the neighboring shanty.

Andy continued making bricks until the sun, and any chance of pursuit, had vanished. Exhausted from the unaccustomed labor he slumped against the unfinished mud wall. The young woman grinned at him awkwardly. She had lit a fire and was baking flat bread on a rounded iron dome. She handed him a flat piece of the *nan* she had baked, then rose smoothly from squatting on her heels. Andy found he was too stiff to move. She giggled at the sight of the young *feringhee* hobbling around like an old man. Andy glared at her, then made motions of needing a wash.

She made him squat over some stones and poured water over his head. The water was cold and Andy scrubbed his body with a worn grey cake of soap. The water ran into his filthy loincloth and he moved uncomfortably, wishing for the pleasure of a *furo*. She crouched by him, looked for a moment at his face, then tugged suggestively at the strip around his loins. The proximity of her hand brought an immediate response, and to his horror he found his cock thickening and lengthening as she unwound the strip from between his thighs.

She looked at the lengthening wet member for a long moment. Her eyes, visibly green even in the light of the kerosene lamp she had procured, were unfathomable. She rose suddenly and headed for the entrance to the unfinished mud shanty. She paused at the door a moment, looking back at Andy over her shoulder. He bit his lip for a moment. If her were to be caught here, with a local woman . . . He shuddered at the thought, but then his balls took over his thinking processes. Before he knew what he was doing, he found himself at the entrance to the hut.

She was lying on her back on the floor on a grimy quilt. She had pulled her pantaloons to her ankles, and her knees were pulled to her chest. In the light of the lantern she had taken he could see that the hair of her mound had been shaved. The long slash of her full cunt beckoned. She peered at him, her luminous eyes rounded over her breasts.

For a long moment he stood there, contemplatively stroking his cock. It rose proudly before him, jutting out like the prow of a ship. She smiled gladly at the display and reciprocated by pulled open the lips of her cunt for his inspection. He knelt before her upraised bum. His hand joined hers at the sweet juicy junction of her legs. His fingers dipped into the honey pot along with hers and she gratefully wiggled her hips to encourage him. He slipped two fingers into her vagina, then added another and another until four fingers of one hand were dipping furiously into her willing flexible orifice.

One of her hands grasped his other hand and guided it to the tiny musky button of her rear entrance. He slid two fingers up her rectum. She gazed at him solemnly from between the circle made by her legs and pantaloons. Gradually the solemnity decreased and her eyes half-closed languorously. Her breathing quickened, keeping time with the sawing of his fingers against her inner tissues. Andy searched for and found the tip of her clitoris with his thumb. She stopped guiding his hands and one of her own went to her skirt. Raising it she exposed pale heavy breasts tipped with rigid broad nipples. She squeezed the mounds mercilessly and her breath began rasping in her throat. He moved harder and she encouraged him, her hands on his shoulders. Gradually they fell into a fast rhythm and her breath rasped even deeper in her throat. Her eyes closed completely and her hips began rubbing forcefully back against his own. She shuddered convulsively and showed her teeth, then growled something when Andy tried to withdraw in order to change position. His fingers inserted in her anus whipped back and forth, and he mauled her doughy breasts hard with his other hand as she had directed him. His own pleasures rose in his balls and she distracted him by the simple expedient of slapping his testicles. Andy cried out, but accepted the hint. He fucked her as strongly as he could, till his muscles burned with fatigue, and his fingers grew stiff. At regular intervals she would sake and quiver, her lips rising over her teeth, her eyes closed. Then, when he had finally given up, and his ardor had began cooling, she suddenly cried out aloud. Her mouth opened and her finger rammed into his rectum painfully, causing his penis to stiffen and shoot a load of plentiful come into her cavernous interior.

She pushed him away silently, rose and offered him a jug of water for his ablutions. They ate together, a poor meal of flat bread wrapped around a stew of lentils. Then she led him outside. "Bus," Andy said, pantomiming driving. She nodded in understanding, and led him to the gate. Before leaving she turned around and regarded the stack of bricks with great satisfaction. They were not terribly well made, but they were made for free, and she was not about to complain. And the foreigner had had other uses as well. All in all she was glad she had saved the *feringhee* from the despicable Pathans.

Andy arrived back in Islamabad late the following morning. The night flight on a rickety small plane had been less than pleasant. After a shower, he had blearily called the airlines. Had Mr. Akebono flown out with them? He had left some documents behind . . . He hit lucky on the third try. Mr. Akebono had flown out the same morning to Amsterdam via Bahrein and Rome. There was apparently no choice. The phial of perfume was on its way to Amsterdam. Andy sighed. He hoped Jim as having more luck.

Finding Mayumi in LA proved to be less of a problem than Jim had anticipated. She had not bothered changing her name, and by pretending to be a harried Japanese travel executive, and speaking bad English and rapid Japanese in turns, he managed to find her hotel. He registered there, to legitimize his presence. Unfortunately for the best of plans, she was out. Gone to Disneyland, that Mecca for Japanese tourists on the West coast. Jim groaned and prepared himself for the worse. Why Disneyland, he did not bother to speculate. He hated the plastic glitz of the place, but he had no choice but to plunge in after his missing rabbit. For a girl on the run Mayumi certainly was not acting in a panic.

Finding a particular party of Japanese in the giant amusement park was not easy. The administration was circumspect and refused to provide information by phone, and at last, in exasperation, Jim headed there himself. After all, Japanese tours tended to be pretty predictable, and easily identifiable by the flag the guide usually carried.

He spotted Mayumi at the entrance to the Pirate's Cave. Jim, who had cajoled his way along the line and managed to find the flag of the tour company she was on, barely had time to leap into the last barge sailing off into the darkness of the ride. He found himself alone in the front seat of the boat with an attractive middle-aged woman from Philadelphia dressed for the occasion in shorts and a halter. She had just lost her husband, and was remarkably cheerful about it. He had last been seen at the Western village. In the dark she crowded close to Jim. The colorful halter she wore barely covered her well-endowed bust and her bare thigh brushed against his.

She did not actually clutch at him until the first drop. As the people behind them screamed happily, she joined in the chorus. Jim did to, as her firm grasp captured his crotch in a surprise raid.

"We're gonna do it boy, right here!" she whispered directly into his ear as the spray spattered them. Curious, and nothing loth, Jim helped recover the initiative by stroking her thigh well up to her shorts. His hands slipped beneath the fabric of her halter. He heard the sound of a zipper, and then her hand was at his crotch. The people behind them screamed in the dark. Her strong hand was inside his fly now, groping for the rising masculinity. She dipped her head in the dark and nipped at the heated plum. Jim squirmed and pulled at her breasts within the halter. She snuggled up to him and one of thighs lifted over his. He found the the zipper on her hot pants extended from front to back, and she wore no panties. Her quim was a moist wetness and she maneuvered herself rapidly until she could sink down onto his waiting pole. He gripped her hips hard and she began bouncing in his lap, emitting squeals and screams of joy that were echoed by the people behind them. As the barge floated along the underground cavern fire spouted at it from all sides. Skeletons rose to frighten them, and rubber pirates cavorted on latex shores. With each new image the other tourists screamed, and with each scream she screamed the loudest, riding Jim's cock to an illimitable series of climaxes.

Jim aided her as best he could, he was laughing hugely as he felt her slick insides sliding up and down his cock. This was the first time he had ever fucked in public before, and in such an uninhibited way no less. He screamed along with her. "It's coming, now, now's the time. Up you Ayooooo," as his sperm bubbled in his balls and rose to flood her interior.

They slumped together in the seat. Her ass was still glued to his. As they started the final ascent she slipped off his lap and zipped up her pants. He did the same and they emerged into candle-lit dark at the top of the tunnel.

She smiled sweetly at him. He could now see here features clearly: an artificial blonde with an unremarkable face. "That was great, wasn't it? I always think the pirates are best, though the mountain ride can be just as thrilling.

She winked at him as they were helped out of the barge. The back of her pants was wet.

"My fifth ride of the day," she said happily, straightening her clothes. "This one with you has been one of the nicest, though they have all been something to treasure." She left no doubt as to her meaning as she swayed away from him.

There was still no sight of Mayumi, and Jim finally gave up the chase and headed for the hotel. Mayumi was not back yet. Retrieving his key he rode the elevator up to his room. He entered the room and headed for the bathroom. His bladder was overflowing.

He saw a movement out of the corner of his eye. He turned and saw a remarkably handsome young woman straightening from the bag, his bag, that lay open on the bed. She stood up, perfectly poised, as if going through someone's luggage was perfectly normal. Jim's heart stopped and his mouth dropped open. Time slowed. There was something terribly familiar about her dark smooth face, but he did not bother to examine the familiarity. The door behind him came open with an effort, he jumped out as she started saying something, and the door slammed just as she reached into her bag. A gun! His mind screamed. He pulled the door forcefully to, flattened against the wall and began running to the elevator. Fortunately for him it was still there. The doors closed behind him just as the young woman came out of his room and started for him. He punched the buttons frenziedly and felt the descent with a wave of relief. She would be unable to shoot at him through the elevator doors.

He charged out of the elevator, fearful of the possibility of her using the stairs. As he leaped out of the lobby, he saw Mayumi standing and talking with two blond strangers. A young man and woman, both dressed conservatively with polite and somehow dreamy smiles on their faces. The woman handed Mayumi something just as Jim leaped down the stairs. "Mayumi," he said breathlessly in Japanese. "They're here. Lets get out, quickly!" he nodded frozenly at the two strangers and led Mayumi at a brisk trot around the corner. Helplessly she followed him, still stunned perhaps by his sudden appearance. He stopped a cab, helped her in, then changed cabs a while later, all the time avoiding her questions, his attention on possible followers.

They ended up in a Chinese restaurant in downtown LA. Jim's face was still pale, and Mayumi looked at him uneasily. He told her briefly of his adventures to date, starting with the latest attack in his hotel room.

For a long minute she looked at him in silence, then her reserve broke. Staring at the table she said "I thought you and Andy were responsible for the attack on me . . ." She started crying. "I was so scared. The *yakuza* threatened me, you see. I did not know if they were following, and so I took the first course. They let me go next to a travel bureau, and I thought if I got away . . . Then I managed to get on a flight to the US. Hiding in the tour was the best I could do. I was afraid to call up the President, because I was responsible for the sample and the tape. And I thought you had set the *yakuza* on me."

"Why should you think that?" he asked.

"I saw Andy talking to the two men who later kidnapped me. He was whistling happily when he got back into the bath. I had gotten up to get some gell for my hair, remember. Why was he whistling if . . ."

"He was scared and didn't want to worry you," Jim said harshly.

"I am sorry," she mumbled. "Where is he now?"

"Chasing after the bloody perfume bottle. Before we left we asked a friend to look after the house. Maybe he has called her. I don't know."

"He is after the perfume?" she half screamed, then started laughing hysterically.

"Why are you laughing," he demanded shaking her roughly.

"Here," she fished in her handbag and extracted a small bottle of commercially sold perfume. "Here it is. When I started suspecting you, I transferred the contents into my empty perfume bottle. The vial has some fruit syrup in it.'' She laughed, nearing hysteria.

He slumped back against the booth. ''Where is the tape then?'' he asked. He had almost forgotten that part of it.

''Here too,'' she smiled tearfully at him. ''They did not know what it was, and forgot it completely.''

''Why did you take it back from me?'' he asked in anguish.

''For the same reason I took the perfume. When those men came to talk to Andy while we were in the bath? I overheard and thought you were in league with them . . . So I took it and ran.''

''Oh hell,'' was all he could say.

''I am sorry Jim-san,'' she said, bowing her head.

''Just a minute, who were those two you were talking to, at the entrance to the hotel?''

''I don't know. They were very nice. They thought I was lost and offered to help, and later, they invited me to a party tonight. Here, they gave me their card.''

''That doesn't add up,'' he said. ''I ran out of the hotel because someone was rifling my luggage. She also tried to shoot me. Now what's this thing.'' He took the card. SUNLIGHT HOUSE, he read. And an address. ''Please come, 8 PM tonight, King' someone had scribbled in pen on the back.

''I must go. They will be very insulted if not . . .''

''Has it occurred to you they are part of our problem? That this is all a set up? That our *yakuza* friends are still after us?''

''Oh no, Jim-san. They are such nice people. It would be very impolite for me to refuse their invitation. And this is America, they couldn't have anything like *yakuza*.''

''Well, if they are the ungodly, we might discover something. So long as we are careful,'' he grumbled.

CHAPTER 14

DUCKS, RABBLE, AND THE SWEET SWEET CANALS

Sunlight House turned out to be a pseudo-ranch house built on extensive grounds close enough to Beverly Hills to quicken heartbeats in any movie goer. Jim thought it garish. Iron gates parted under the scrutiny of an invisible guardian as he presented the card Mayumi had received to a video eye. They drove up a winding road through an artificial forest which hid the house itself from the road. "King" was there to greet them, not at all put out by Mayumi's guest. Jim, suspicious as always and a product of California himself, put on his dumb Jap act. That consisted chiefly of smiling nervously, bowing at every third word, uttering "hai, hai" frequently, and pretending an astonishing degree of ignorance for a man of his age and assumed culture. *Gaijin* he had noticed before, lapped it up. Somehow it never occurred to *gaijin* that modern Japanese were capable of the duplicity their fathers were supposedly famous for, and he exploited that attitude to the full.

King was dressed in a caftan-like robe over designer jeans. He introduced Happiness, a Junoesque blonde Californian with a smile as nauseatingly sweet and a complexion as carefully brown as toffee.

She hooked her arms into Jim's and led him away. King

did the same with Mayumi, and they were ushered into the cool darkness of a large living room. It was occupied by a large bunch of people eating, drinking and making passes. Among them circulated a number of other people dressed in the caftan and jeans that seemed to be the common Sunlight House uniform. A terrace, bordered with thick bushes was open to the public. There were tables with drinks. Several doors led out of the large room. Over one of them was a banner HAPPINESS AND BRIGHTNESS: SUNLIGHT HOUSE.

"Have you heard of Sunlight House before?" Happiness asked cheerfully.

"Ah . . . Sunrito House? *Koko ne*?"

She pantomimed energetically "This is Sunlight House. We are dedicating ourselves to bringing sunlight into every heart. Good people. We bring love and happiness."

"*Ah, so desu ka? Rove you rike*?" Jim stared lecherously and obviously at her mammary endowments which she had practically shoved at him as if to emphasize the concept of love. "I rove. I rike rove," Jim pantomimed, stroking the air in front of her bosom.

The blonde goddess laughed and moved slightly away. But not too far. "Then you must join us. Sunlight House is *about* love. And happiness of course."

"You Happiness, no? I rove Happiness" he bowed and simultaneously reached for her ramparts.

She chuckled artificially, nimbly avoiding his hands. Obviously he had misunderstood, only to be expected with such poor English. "Later, perhaps, after you have joined us and have heard the lecture by our Master. Would you like something to eat? Drink? We also have some other substances," she lowered her voice and whispered coyly into his ear.

"Ah! Marijuana!" Jim said gaily and loudly. "I rike. Carifornia yes? Rove yes? Rove happiness!" and beamed at her. He regretted he did not have round framed glasses to beam through: he would have loved to go into his Mr. Moto impersonation.

"I'll be right back," she smiled again, a flash of capped teeth in the brown tan, and walked away, going through the door under the banner. Another one of the elect, in his caftan and jeans came up to engage Jim in conversation. Mayumi had been engaged in conversation with King and another of the elect at another corner of the room, and Jim made his excuses and turned to look for her. There were about fifty people in the room constantly shifting around, and it took him some time to discover that she was not anywhere in the room. He tried some of the other doors. All were locked except the one under the banner, and when he tried that he found himself restrained by a large hand on his shoulder. He turned to face two big men. Both gave the impression of massive crew-cut blondness, even the coffee-colored one among the two. They smiled at Jim artificially. "That is only for the adepts, I'm afraid," one of them, the darker one said.

"A so sorry. My furende she go. Where?"

Tweedledum and Tweedledee looked at one another for a moment. "She was with the Master?"

"Master? Ah so sorry. Not know. Mista Kingu, you know?"

"That is me," the other one said.

"No. So sorry." Jim grinned with all his teeth, still bowing and trying the door handle. The door opened behind his back. Happiness stepped out.

"Why, Mr. Suzuki," she said brightly. "Come, must hear the Master, the Reverend King King." The partying group was shushed. A spotlight went on at the far end of the room where a dark alcove had been avoided by everyone. The caftan-dressed members straightened, raised their hands above their heads. A man appeared and seated himself in an armchair. He smiled genially. He was as tanned and plastic as his subordinates, otherwise completely ordinary. He waved everyone to a seat, then began to speak.

Jim listened to the words which appeared to be a mixture of self-help, new-age, and mystical notions cribbed from half a dozen crackerjack cults and sects. After about ten minutes of that the Master turned them over to his assistant, Mz Joy, who proved to be so similar in appearance to Happiness that Jim had to turn his head to see that Happiness was still standing by his side. The feel of her warm thigh, the touch of her full breasts upon his arm convinced him that they were indeed two women.

Mayumi had passed through the main room, guided lightly but firmly by King's bulk. He had offered her a drink, some sort of fruit punch spiked with alcohol, and they had listened for a short while to one of the caftan-clad acolytes as he expounded to a small group of visitors. It was clear that about half of those present had arrived at the party by the same means she had. There were several Japanese scattered among the crowd, most, she guessed from overhearing their conversation, had been invited by King or someone like him.

She was delighted by the friendliness everyone displayed, by the looseness and relaxation of her hosts. The punch warmed her insides, and the last of the fear that had taken hold of her in Tokyo evaporated with the evening. She searched for Jim with her eyes, saw him indulging in what appeared to be a very intimate conversation. She envied the blonde beauty her impressive breastworks, but otherwise was relieved that Jim with his gloomy fears seemed happily occupied.

"Would you like to see the Master?" King whispered in her ear. His warm breath tickled her ear.

"The Master? I thought you were the host . . ."

"Oh no," King whispered through the sounds of the party. "Master King, our leader, is your host. Would you like to meet him?" There was a curious, somehow repellent fervor and intensity in his voice. Mayumi did not know enough foreigners to be able to tell whether this was normal or not. In any case, good manners dictated she go. As did her curiosity.

"Of course I will come."

He led her through the banner-marked doorway. They walked down a narrow passageway lined with doors.

Through one of them which was only partly closed she could hear rustlings, and sounds which indicated a person or persons engaged in great muscular effort.

They walked through another door, then another, finally arriving in a large dimly lit room. It was divided into alcoves and lit by a single skylight. Each alcove was padded and contained several large cushions. A woman and four men were sitting in one alcove. They all wore caftans, but no jeans. One of them who was obviously the head of the group, wore a large golden solar disk on his breast. He smiled at her as King made the introductions. He was indeed Master King King, head of Sunlight House.

A sudden snort, as if a giant animal had appeared at her side made Mayumi jump. Master King made an annoyed face. "Have that air intake fixed." He turned to Mayumi. "I'm sorry. The mansion was built on solar principles, but not too well. The cool air enters through the central well, but we've had to supplement it with a pump, which makes the noise."

"You are cousins?" she looked from King to King King.

The Master laughed gently. "No. We are all King. Those who join us—I hope we will number you among them, my dear—are all reborn into the light, and we give them the name King to mark their ascent. Women we of course call Joy, or Happiness."

The young woman at his side, her long hear spread on her breast, smiled and nodded agreement.

"Won't you join us?" King King asked.

They were all soon chatting amiably. Mayumi had to make up a story about her presence in LA and about her job, but enjoyed herself thoroughly. Drinks and some snacks were served. She thought the organic processed bran meal awful, but ate it out of politeness.

"It is such a lovely country you come from," King King said, his hand stroking her leg lightly. "I would love to go there some time."

"And such charming women. Is everyone as beautiful

as yourself?'' Joy, or Happiness leaned forward, her lips moist. Her caftan fell open displaying a pair of large suntanned breasts. Mayumi looked on appreciatively and somewhat apprehensively. One of the Kings who was sitting at Joy or Happiness's feet stroked her long legs absently as he reached for a snack. He smiled up into Mayumi's face as he did so. She felt her nipples harden. She smiled back at him, then noticing the predatory looks on the others' faces, smiled at them all. She thought she knew what they had in mind, and was not opposed to the idea.

King King rose suddenly. ''I have to go about my duties for a little while. I will be right back my child. Will you wait for me?''

She smiled back at him in assent and he leaned down, placed a hand on each of her shoulders and kissed her deeply. ''I like to have happiness around me. My acolytes will show you.'' He swirled away and was gone. Mayumi looked up to see that the other alcoves were filling with people. Most of them wore the caftan's that marked their membership in the group. The others wore street clothes. A humming rose from around them as they mouthed some sort of hymn.

Joy leaned over and kissed Mayumi. Her mouth tasted of mints. The Kings' crowded around her, stroking her body lightly but firmly.

Mayumi felt her own lust thrill her insides. Orgies were no mystery to her, though she preferred her partners to allow her more freedom of action. The Kings were crowding around her and their caresses became more insistent. Hands snaked between her legs, undid her clothes, visited the warmth of her body. A head thrust itself between her legs and she felt a trained tongue lick at her panties. She spread her legs to facilitate entry and was unsurprised to find Joy leaning over her, her caftan open and inviting. Mayumi fondled the full fruit, delighting in their smoothness and size. Joy smiled encouragingly. ''It will be a wonderful production,'' she said.

''Production?''

''Of course. The Master is preparing a catalog of our activities. We are filming now. When he returns, he and you will be the stars of the show.''

Mayumi looked up and carefully peered at the other alcoves. What she had taken to be a hymn of some sort, proved to be mixed with low-voiced instructions to the crews of at least three cameras whose bright lenses were directed at her.

''Oh no. *Ikenai*!'' She said furiously, changing to Japanese in her outrage. ''You stop!''

''Don't worry,'' one of the Kings tried to sooth her. ''You are part of the great experiment, part of Sunlight House now. We will make a documentary to advertise our activities.''

She tried to struggle, tried to rise, but the press of bodies around her was too strong, the four people too determined. A mouth was sucking at each of her breasts now, and the head between her legs was replaced by another while she could feel one of the King's masturbating against her leg. Under other circumstances she would have felt flattered, but at the moment she was mad enough to strike out against those trying to impose their will on her.

Master King King was suddenly standing before her. His caftan rose in an obvious bulge before him. He smiled down upon her, raised his hands to the sky while intoning a benediction to which everyone answered. Joy/Happiness rose from her place by Mayumi's head and pulled off his caftan. His rigid penis extended in a bow before his belly. He smiled at Mayumi and said ''Let it roll!'' as he knelt between her parted legs and sought for her liquid cunt with his hand.

Mayumi struck at the man beside her, then struck again. She threw her handbag at the one on her other side. It missed, and its contents scattered, some of them hitting in the sound of glass.

Laughing, they overpowered her and Master King King

thrust up at her. She felt the warmth of his erection pierce her wet nether lips. Her hips responded automatically and she raised herself higher to permit entry. The smell of sex was in her nostrils and in any case, she was ready.

Master King King roared as he sank deeper into the exquisite tiny oriental beauty before him. "She's so tight!" he screamed, and Mayumi, allowing herself liberties she had never allowed herself before, struck at him, then struck again. The pain seemed to have no effect on him. His hips pumped wildly at her, and she could feel the slap of his balls against her buttocks.

The coordinated attack on her lost its focus. The Kings on either side were no longer hampering her. Instead they were intent on their own affairs. Happiness or Joy was easing herself, her mouth grunting happily, onto an erect prick. Another of the King's was excitedly masturbating between her full breasts. A third, tired of waiting his turn, was grappling with one of the camera crew. She fell to the padded floor of the alcove and sought eagerly for the penetration of his flesh. The camera crashed after her. The other camera crews were suddenly similarly involved, unable to keep their hands off one another.

Mayumi rose to go. In one of the alcoves three men were noisily enjoying one woman. Their faces were blind to everything. A second woman was lying dazed on the floor, her hand between her legs, a look of bliss on her face. Two women were struggling over one man in a second alcove. He had his hand deeply inside one of them while his cock was being jerked by the other one's hands into a state of readiness. Mayumi adjusted her skirt, passing a hand between her legs to collect the moisture there then wiping the signs of his own lust into King King's bloody hair. She had hit him as hard as she could with one of the plates, otherwise he would still be pumping at her. Giddily she staggered to the door, almost unable to control her own lust, wanting only to join the fun.

The lecturer who had held the party spellbound seemed bemused by her own words, and there was evidence of restlessness in the crowd. Her oration stumbled, and the entire audience seemed excited as she stroked the length of her own body unconsciously. Surprisingly, the caftan-draped acolytes seemed restless too.

Without warning Jim found himself engulfed by Happiness. She bore him backwards onto the floor. Her heavy breasts, tanned without any bikini marks, tumbled into his hands. Her mouth was on his, at his ear, his neck, then working its way downwards. He was reacting to her heavy scented presence and she exclaimed joyfully at the presence of his erection. He peered over her blonde head. The greying lecturer had thrown off her caftan. She had flattened breasts that were being fondled not too gently by two of the guests. The large prick of one of the Kings was poised before her mouth and it was obvious she was ready to accept it. Beneath her a tubby little man, one of the guests, was tripping his hips into hers with the speed of an air hammer. Jim could see the sweat break out on her brow, and the tiny scars near her nose and on her chin practically glinted as moisture collected along them. The last glimpse he got of her was when her lips opened wide and the broad ruby head of her acolyte was inserted fully, extending the flesh near her throat.

Happiness had reached her goal and Jim's erection sprung free. She cried out in delight and mounted him. He peered down while fondling her full breasts and she parted her bush for their mutual convenience. Jim watched entranced as first the head and then the entire shaft disappeared into her body. She looked up triumphantly, then drew herself to his chest, mashing her full jugs onto the young man beneath her. He started what he thought would be a slow delicious movement up her channel, but the woman perched on him was too impatient. She bucked herself rapidly onto his erection, gluing her lips to his. Occasionally she would vary the rhythm and her hips would make broad circles and figure eights over Jim's loins. Her sweat was dripping into his face and his hands were running up and down her back. He felt something wet there. Two men were engaged with a woman nearby. One of them, who had been bucking into her from behind and reached a crescendo. As his cock spurted he missed his mark and his large dark cock spurted drops which flew like shot, sprinkling the woman's buttocks and flying off to spatter Happiness. The woman he was in paid no attention. Her head was in another man's lap and he was gasping as she skillfully swallowed his rod to the roots. Noticing that the man inserted in her cunt had stopped moving she raised her head. Without missing a beat she swapped ends, seating herself on the erection she had been treating with her mouth, and sucking lustfully at the uncoordinated hose-owner.

The sights and sounds of the developing orgy, and the pressures exerted on his prick by Happiness's skilful and enthusiastic actions brought Jim to a climax much sooner than he would have liked. He leaped like a salmon, driving himself impossibly high into Happiness's welcoming depths. She shrieked as she bore her full weight down onto the impaling member, then they both collapsed back onto the floor as wave after wave of electrifying sensation swept through their bodies.

They lay clasped together, moving just slightly while Jim's cream leaked out of her hole and down their thighs. "Excuse me," a polite voice interrupted them. "May I?" Happiness raised her head to face a thick erection, still moist and sticky from its previous encounter. She rose to the occasion, stuffing her mouth greedily with the offered gift, scraping her teeth carefully along the under side. The bearded man above her gave a grunt of approval. His hips jutted forward and his enormous ball bag swung contentedly at the base. Jim suddenly remembered Mayumi. He had a good idea what had started the current action, and it occurred to him that it might be a signal, a request for help. He slid out from under Happiness, who promptly lay on her back for the convenience of Big-balls, and slithered through the press in the direction of the bannered door.

Mayumi found Jim battering at the locked door through which she had entered the Master's den. She grasped at him, running her hands excitedly over his hard body. Under his pants he had an enormous erection.

''No time for that,'' he groaned. ''They've all gone crazy out there.''

They had indeed. Couples, triples, and larger groups were tied together in urgently moving knots, giving free play to their pleasure.

Jim was tempted to rejoin them, but he had more important things on his mind. ''What happened to you?''

Mayumi giggled drunkenly. ''They tried to make me star in a porn movie.''

''How did you get away?'' Jim asked horrified. His eyes were still on the milling developing orgy around him.

She giggled again, still under the influence of liquor and SuccSex. ''I broke the vial of SuccSex. Next to the airconditioner intake.'' She giggled and reached for him. ''Serve them right, don't you think?''

Jim had to agree.

''I want you now,'' she said simply.

''I'm afraid Happiness has taken it all out of me,'' he muttered. ''Besides, we had better get out of here. Here, take the keys to the car. I'll delay them if there's any pursuit. You must call up my father and tell him that you are OK, otherwise he'll go on blaming me and Andy.''

She sobered somewhat at the thought, and accepted the keys to the rented car. He convoyed her to the door. The two Sunlight House members who had hovered at all times near the exit were gone. One of them was lying on the floor, a middle aged female guest holding his handle firmly between her teeth. He seemed none the worse for the experience and was making no attempt to escape. The other doorkeeper was nowhere to be seen. Mayumi slipped out and Jim turned back to the party. He wanted badly to join, instead he had to content himself with visual appreciation.

The effects of SuccSex took some time to wear off. By

that time the orgy had gotten into a momentum all its own. Jim took careful mental notes, on the assumption that a field test of the new product would help alleviate some of Lenny's ire.

He grinned happily to himself and turned to the punch bowl as a blonde young woman tugged at his leg. Just as he was about to fall into temptation again, he saw two burly figures exit the banner-marked doorway and move purposefully through the crowd in his direction, ignoring all temptation. A third figure slid into the room from the outside and followed intently behind the first two. Jim gulped. The two males were undoubtedly muscle. And the third was the woman who had tried to assassinate him in his hotel.

Jim hoped Mayumi had made her getaway already, because it was now time to leave. "Feets, do your stuff," he muttered.

A bemused black head raised itself from between pale blonde curl-topped thighs. " 'Feet', not 'feets'," the black man said pedantically in cultivated Ivy League tones. There was a picture of bulldog in blue on his sweatshirt—the only thing he wore—and for a moment before he took off Jim wished for a real bulldog by his side.

He reached the door several leaps before the goons, and sped off into the dark. What he needed was a place to hide. The goons may well not belong to either Clouds and Rain *nor* the Typhons. But they were very definitely goons, and the best course was to lay low. He needed somewhere soft and unexpected. At least until Mayumi could get back to Kiso and explain things to the President and Vice-President of Clouds and Rain Corporation. Then some of the heat would be off . . . His foster family, the Suzukis perhaps? But he had no desire to put them into danger, if there was any around. In LA itself? But he knew no one, and anyone who knew the city would be able to flush him out of a hotel or motel. He ran down the drive, climbed nimbly over the gate, and found himself after a few breathtaking minutes near a shopping mall.

Two days of skulking around in motels and changing his room each night wore rapidly on his nerves. He tried to read, to watch TV, and every once in a while, to call Mineko at his house in Tokyo. He hoped Mayumi had made it back to Tokyo, and had contacted Kitty and Lenny, but noon had called Mineko, and he was afraid to call Clouds and Rain himself. The fear of the female assassin was still upon him, and every dark-haired girl he passed made his knees turn to jelly.

He went out late at night to get something to eat. Slim female figures passing by naturally led his imagination in directions he did not want to go. With Mayumi back in Japan, Mineko there too, and some other female stalking him, he was about to lose his mind, not knowing whether to come on to every chick he saw passing by, or turn and flee from them.

A cosmetics billboard caught his eye and tickled something in memory, but his mind was too fogged with lust to function. Then suddenly the two sensations, the idea of cosmetics and the feel of lust came together in his mind. There was one place he could probably hide in comfort, in great comfort. He knew, he now remembered, only one person in LA. Her name was May McCormick, and she had developed a passion for Jim and Andy, had helped them, in fact, when they were searching for their fathers, Kitamura and Fine. He scrabbled through his address book, then made a hurried call to his house in Tokyo. There was still no message from Andy on the machine, and he hurriedly recorded a guarded one himself. He would have to get May alone, and calling in the middle of the night was not a good way to do it. Her husband—Harry, or Henry—would probably be at home.

Jim spent the rest of the night moving cautiously from one all-night diner to another. His paranoia was exacerbated by the usual sounds of American city life—sirens, cars squealing, the occasional gunshot—which made him dart about nervously. Every movement brought visions of gang members, muggers, and the invisible shadow of his pursuers. Afraid to return to his motel, he longed for the security and comfort of Tokyo, and if not that, at least the warmth of May's body.

Andy found a hotel not far from Damm square. The summer was almost over and the streets and squares were almost empty of the millions of scruffy and not-so-scruffy tourists that infested the beautiful city. Andy took some time to familiarize himself, and soon discovered the raunchy red-light district to be right behind his hotel, stretching away towards the railway station. It was early afternoon. Few of the lamps were lit, but some of the professionals were already preparing themselves for the evening's work. There was a bewildering array of color, shape and size. It seemed that the city ordinances required *some* covering, for all were slightly covered by odd pieces of cloth at strategic places. Good professionals as they were, they smiled invitingly at the prospective customer as Andy passed by. He was fascinated, yet somehow repelled, by the aseptic commercialism it demonstrated.

Finding Akebono was going to be much more difficult in Holland than in Pakistan. Japanese tourists were ubiquitous in Amsterdam. Shops catered to them, as did restaurants, tour guides, and the beauties of the red light district. For one brief joyous moment Andy considered starting there, then his sense prevailed. A detective agency would be a better bet.

A kiosk yielded a Paris-based Herald Tribune. He looked at the classified, none of which said anything about detective agencies. A Dutch newspaper was next. He flipped it open trying to puzzle out the polysyllabic Dutch sentences. Disgusted at his inability to comprehend the language, he closed it again. A picture caught his attention. A group of policemen were huddled around a man whose bedraggled face was to the camera. The face was familiar.

He looked at the newspaper again. The photograph showed the body of a man looking suspiciously like Akebono being fished out of a canal. He couldn't make out a single word. He puzzled over the complicated Dutch words for a long moment, then said "Damn!" loudly, and started to crumple the paper up.

"I *beg* your pardon!" A disapproving voice said behind him.

He turned sideways. A young woman, her long blonde hair hanging loose was looking at him with raised eyebrows.

"I'm sorry," he said. "I was just upset . . . Ah, a minute please miss. You speak English?" His obvious confusion and concern did more to assuage her feelings than his brief apology.

"Most Dutch my age can," she said, smiling to take the sting out of her words.

"I hate to bother you," he said self-consciously "But could you perhaps read this for me? Please?"

His obvious distress was plain to see, and she smiled agreement.

"Tourist attacked . . . Do you want me to read everything?"

"Just the gist," he begged.

"The tourist, he is from Japan. He was attacked. He fought back. Another man, a Dutchman was injured. He is known to the police as drug-dealer. This Japanese, police say he is not just tourist but *yakeza*. I'm sorry, I don't understand the word. Maybe you do?"

Andy nodded briefly. His eyes were fixed on her lips, anxious not to miss a word. "*Yakuza*," he said absently. She had lovely mobile lips, he noted.

"The Dutchman also in canal says the Japanese cheated him. He gave bottle of substance . . ., That is newspaper euphemism for drugs," she added, pursing her lips in disapproval, ". . . but it was only fruit juice."

Andy's jaw dropped. "Fruit juice?" he exploded. Other patrons in the brown cafe turned to look at him with disapproval. "Fruit juice? Are you sure?"

She reread the paragraph again carefully. "No, not

juice. Fruit concentrate. Syrup. Fruit concentrate to mix with water.''

He stared at her incredulously, then to her alarm his face started to change. He started laughing helplessly, barely able to keep his seat. ''Fruit juice? I've been chasing a bottle of *fruit juice* around the world?'' He had to grip his ribs hard to stop the peals of mirth. One of the patrons moved uneasily away. There were tears of laughter in Andy's eyes and he rocked to and fro muttering ''Fruit juice, fruit juice!''

''Did they say what flavor?'' he asked, then had to try and control his laughter again as the blonde girl reread the article solemnly, then said ''No. No flavor.''

''I'm sorry,'' Andy said. ''I'm really sorry I laughed. It was more out of relief than anything else. He, that man, stole the bottle from a friend of mine, and I've been trying to get it back. I did not know there was juice in it. Akebono didn't either obviously. I wonder what happened to . . .''

''You are selling drugs?'' she said in outrage.

''No, no.'' Andy protested, and gave her a brief resume of his story. She laughed delightedly. ''I hope this is all true,'' she said.

''Oh, it is, it is. Look, you have been wonderful. Can I invite you to lunch?''

Trudy was a charming companion, as he discovered over lunch, with a well-developed sense of humor, and a knowledge of her native Amsterdam, which she knew as if it were a tiny village. She was a student at one of the universities, and as their meal ended, she started looking at her watch more frequently.

''A class?'' he asked as he paid the bill.

''No. I have a job. To get me through college. I must go now.''

He kissed her lightly and she responded in a friendly but not encouraging manner. ''If you're ever in Japan,'' he said. ''Come and visit. Here, this is my card. I owe you a big one.''

She smiled, waved, was swallowed in the crowd of afternoon shoppers and walkers around the square.

Andy found a telephone and called Tokyo. He was whistling as the phone rang. He hoped Jim was as successful, and wondered what had happened to the real vial, though he thought he could make a shrewed guess. The message on the answering machine was perplexing. "Meet me in May," was all Jim's voice said.

Andy pondered. Suddenly the message was clear. May it would be, though he wondered why the secrecy. He hurried off to make arrangements to fly to LA.

The clerk suggested that the best way to get to Schipohl airport was by train. Andy headed north wandering along the canals and heading in the general direction of the train station. Evening was falling and he had no luggage beyond a shoulder bag he had acquired at the last minute in Narita.

As he walked he looked at the house fronts, regretting that he did not have more time to explore the beautiful city. Most of the buildings looked as if they had been built as residences. Three or four storeys of windows overlooked the street. He reached one house the windows of which glowed red. Like Christmas decorations, he thought. Drawing level with the house he automatically peered in. A woman stared back at him. She was practically naked, dressed in a tiny G-string and halter that emphasized rather than hiding her charms. She smiled at him and beckoned. He smiled back and winked, then indicated his watch. He would have loved to respond to her suggestion but had two hours to get to Schipohl, and no idea how long the pre-boarding procedures would take. She shrugged and he moved on.

Trudy was sitting in the next window. She wore tiny bikini panties and long stockings, a lace bra that did nothing to hide her generous breasts, and a smile. The smile, though not the rest of her clothing dropped as she saw Andy passing by and staring fully at her. Then the smile was back on her face, as false as the pasties on her neighbor's nipples.

It took a supreme effort of will for Andy to behave naturally. He smiled at her gaily, waved unconcernedly at her as if he had just met an acquaintance on the street. Her momentary embarrassment passed though she made no effort to entice him into her parlor. The show-window was sealed, and probably soundproofed. He tapped his watch and wiggled his hands to indicate a plane, then mouthed "Tokyo! See you soon," waved her good bye.

She smiled then, an honest smile which lit up her face, and waved good bye. Someday, perhaps, they would meet again.

CHAPTER 15

IS IT MAY AGAIN?

Jim sneaked uneasily into the garden around May's house. He examined the name over the bell carefully, spinning around at every sound as if expecting to be overtaken at any moment. Dissatisfied, her sneaked through the shrubbery to the other side of the house, and knocked gently, then louder, at the kitchen door.

"Who is it?" the voice was definitely feminine, and it sounded like May's but who could be sure?

"Jim," he whispered.

"Who?" The voice was sharply suspicious now.

"May, open the door," he whispered somewhat more loudly. "Its Jim. Let me in."

The kitchen door opened a crack and one suspicious eye peered at him. Then the door was flung open and she stood there, warm and full, her mouth and the neck of her frilly peignoir open.

He slipped through the door and closed it quickly behind him. "Is there anyone here? besides you, I mean?"

"No. Henry is on a business trip . . ."

He held her hand and rushed her through the house to the front, and peered through the curtains onto the street.

"Just relax. Calm down . . ." May's blonde curls bobbed with her voice. "What's the matter?"

''Someone is out to kill me,'' Jim said his voice unsteady. He had managed to work himself by quick stages into a state of absolute panic.

She wet her lips, checked the front door locks then pulled him to a seat. ''Tell me more about it?''

''I don't know,'' he said, his eyes still darting nervously to the door, though he was starting to catch his breath. ''It all started with the Clouds and Rain Co., you remember?'' He told her the story of his trip with Andy to Kiso and of their discoveries there, then of his more recent adventures. ''So I don't know what has happened to Andy. I left him a message to meet me here, I thought you could help us. At least, you're the only one I know in the LA area.'' He turned to look at her for the first time, taking in the full pink breast showing fully under her neckline and sensing the warmth of her body. ''And certainly someone I would have wanted to see in any case.''

''You had better call your apartment in Tokyo again, to see that Andy is all right,'' she said pragmatically, ignoring the hand he had placed on her knee as he talked.

''There'll be plenty of time to do that later,'' he said. Some of his confidence was returning. He bent his head and kissed the visible breast while fishing out its twin from beneath the pale blue fabric. She gasped with delight. Jim knew her weakness was her breasts, and he exploited the weakness to the full.

''But he's your brother,'' she murmured.

''There's nothing I can do,'' he said. ''Until later.''

May was panting now. Her head was thrown back as Jim nibbled delicately at the pale skin of her breasts. He sank down into an available armchair and seated her full ass on his knees. She pulled his head to her breasts and he obligingly raised each full jug and nibbled at the underside, something he knew she liked.

Her dress slid off her shoulders and he increased the pressure of his lips and mouth. His hand descended to her waist and she opened her legs obligingly. His fingers burrowed between the petals of her cunt and a warm musky scent rose between their bodies.

She felt his cock. It was stiffly erect, ready for anything. She hoped she would not have to tell him what to do, but they had been occasional lovers for some time, and she had great hopes. Her only real regret was that Andy was absent.

Jim rose precipitously and the spilled to the floor, landing on top of her. He rose to sit over her, and hastily slipped out of his clothes. Leaning forward he placed his erect prick in the valley between her breasts. She pulled them together and he began a long shafting of the delicious soft mounds. The plum-shaped dark tip emerged from the pale hills, threatening her face. May reached for his clothes, bundled them and placed them under her head. Each time he shoved forward now the tip of this cock reached her lips and she licked quickly at the salty drops of fluid that had gather there. The feel of his silky length against the skin of her breasts was exquisite and she hoped it would go on forever. But she could tell by the preliminary jerkings of his shaft and by the rapid movements that thrummed against her chest that he was ready to erupt. She clutched her breasts more tightly. Staring into her eyes Jim helped her pleasure by squeezing her breasts together. One of her hands dipped between her legs and she stimulated her clitoris and vaginal channel with her hands. She too fund herself swept along in a tide of mounting passion just as his breathing began quickening.

"What the *hell* do you think you're doing?"

The familiar male voice breaking into her activities made May jar Jim off his stride. Jim fell to the carpet beside her, instinctively trying to rise and cover his cock at the same time.

"You bastard!" The voice called out in rage.

Jim gulped.

"Couldn't you wait for me?" Andy inquired, unbuttoning his shirt hurriedly.

"Where did you come from?" Jim stammered.

"Back door. Lots of prowlers about, May dear. You should be more careful."

She giggled, then started laughing uproariously. Andy, then Jim joined her.

She rose to a seated position, conscious of her nudity, and of the fact that these two young men enjoyed and loved her body, even though it was past its prime. "The bedroom is upstairs. This carpet is rough on my back."

They walked up the broad stairs carrying their clothes. Andy slipped a hand over one full quivering buttock and stroked the crack of her ass familiarly. Jim's hand was between her legs, his finger poking into her juicy cunt.

"Just like old times," she whispered, then kissed each one briefly before entering her bedroom.

"How did you make out with the *yakuza*?" Jim asked, suddenly reminded that there were more serious things afoot.

"All settled," Andy said, laughing. "There was nothing in the vial."

"Oh yeah. I know that. Mayumi told me she had switched the contents . . ."

"And you didn't tell me?" Andy yelped. "Where did you find her anyway?"

"How could I tell you?" Jim argued. "In any case, though I found Mayumi, there's still some trouble. Someone's trying to kill me." He repeated his story for the second time.

"It just doesn't make sense,' Andy mummbled. His face was a study in frustration.

"Hey, later boys, OK?" May was standing close to them and the warmth and delight of her body was enough to distract them from their troubles.

The bedroom was large, dominated by an wide bed covered with rumpled silk sheets. The wall behind the bed consisted of a large mirror. A huge walk-in closet, almost a room in its own right, held a selection of expensive dresses and furs.

She backed to the bed, pulling both men with her, then

lay down and opened her legs. "Lie on me, both of you," she whispered, mounding her full breasts as high as she could. "You know what I like. Fuck them! Screw my tits. Come on, fuck them." Her hands squeezed the full pale breasts exacting a pink blush.

The two young men mounted her cautiously on either side, their cocks burrowing into her melons. She peered down at her two breasts, admiring the contrast between the two cocks, one brown and purple, the other pinker.

"Fuck, fuck," she urged them, and Jim and Andy began jabbing their cocks at her full jugs as she nibbled at their bellies. She started moaning as the pleasurable feel of two male members screwing her most sensitive spot and greatest delight overcame her inhibitions. Both men had been without a woman for several days, and their passion rose at a pace with hers.

She spilled them off her suddenly, made them lie side by side then crouched over them. In that position both her breasts hung free. Rolling over to their sides as she knew they would, they returned to poking her breasts from either side. She was crying aloud now, her eyes closed and her breathing spasmodic. Andy slid his free hand along her body, stroking her flanks. Then he pulled at her full buns, dipping his fingers into the crack while Jim pulled from the other side. His finger tickled her tight rear hole as he was conscious of Jim inserting fingers into her waiting box. She moaned again and her ass started a shafting motion against the intruding fingers.

She rose to a squat on the broad bed. Jim and Andy knelt on either side, pounding her swaying breasts forcefully with their erections. Jim raised her breast and inserted his cock under the full fleshy perfect breast. He started fucking deeply into the breast. May practically screamed when Andy started doing the same thing. All three of them were close now. Waves of orgasm washed through May's body, but she wanted more and more, which the twins were supplying her with. The three of them clutched one another, long stiff pricks jammed into soft feminine curves and she cried out again, nibbling and sucking at the hard male breasts as her own soft ones were fucked to delirious heights.

The two men stiffened against her, and she fought their withdrawal knowing the end was near. Andy grasped his prick with his fist and mashed it into her broad pink nipple. Jim beat at her breast with his own fleshy cudgel. Both male faces were contorted with uncontrollable muscular rictuses. Squirts of translucent cream shot out of each man and covered each breast. They were overlaid by arabesques of more fluid as both men sprayed her mammaries. She held onto the cocks, rubbing the softening members into the greater softness of her own breasts. Her nipples gave a final jerk and the waves of her own orgasm subsided. They collapsed on to the bed, May gratefully stroking their heaving sides. Gradually their eyes closed and they fell asleep, still entwined.

"Ms. McCormick?" There was a tremulous voice on the stairway.

May sat up in bed, her full breasts still sticky with their dried come jouncing merrily. "Oh my God," she whispered. "Its Jo Ann!! I invited her here, fool that I am. She mustn't see you like that. She's so stupid she's bound to tell Henry."

She motioned hurriedly to the wide open closet, and the two young men leaped inside, pulling the door to. "I'm just having a shower," May called out as she left the bed and hurriedly reorganized it. "Make yourself comfortable downstairs dear." She vanished into the bathroom and a few seconds later they could hear the water start.

"Should we get dressed?" Jim whispered into Andy's ear while peering through the slats in the closet door.

"Might as well," Andy whispered back.

Just then they were interrupted. A tall, rather thin girl in jeans, cowboy boots and a rather skimpy top wandered into the room. She looked about her curiously, her eyes wide open. She pried into everything, starting with the sheets on the wide double-bed which she fingered enviously, then to the large makeup dresser, touching everything lightly and enviously. She opened May's dresser, and cautiously touched the underthings and boxes of jewelry within. Gradually she approached the closet and the two brothers shrank back between fur coats and formal dresses. The sound of the shower abruptly stopped, but Jo Ann was so intent on her examination that she noticed nothing. She opened the closet, letting light in, and stroked a mink coat that hanged before her face. The brother's stilled their breathing, wondering what to do.

"Jo Ann!" May said in surprise and some alarm. Jo Ann spun around. She took in May's full body, barely covered by a large and fluffy towel. Her breathing quickened and she took one uncertain step towards May. "What are you doing here? I thought you'd wait for me downstairs as I asked."

"I'm sorry,' the younger woman said. "I didn't hear what you said. I was worried for you, I thought I heard a man's voice, so I came up to investigate." Her eyes were intent on the tops of May's breasts. May suddenly became aware that her towel was slipping. For some reason this caused her embarrassment and she pulled the fabric higher. Jo Ann's eyes promptly shifted to her crotch and May realized that what she had gained in the high she had lost in the low. Jo Ann took two rapid steps towards her. Her thin hands went out and hovered before May's breasts.

"Oh Mz McCormick. May. You're so lovely." Her breath was coming in short gasps. "You know why I had to leave Omaha?" The mid-West twang was strong in her throat. "It was because, . . . because . . . They're so *stuffy* over there. You and Mr. McCormick were so nice to let me stay. I had a friend, we . . . we . . . You're so beautiful," she whispered. Her hands moved a fraction forward and they rested on May's towel covered nipples. May said nothing and Jo Ann took that as gesture of encouragement. She squeezed the full mounds slightly, and May's eyes half-closed. Jo Ann dropped to her knees before the older blonde. She sniffed deeply at the damp dark pussy hairs and the prominent soft lips, then buried her mouth in the mound, crying incoherently. May looked down at the girl, open mouthed. She started to say something, then saw Jim and Andy, both still naked, grinning at her from the closet. She blushed, and Jim blew her a kiss. She dropped the towel on Jo Ann's head, spreading her legs slightly to keep the girl busy and allow the two men a chance to escape. They laughed silently and made no move to dress and leave. Instead, Andy mouthed "encourage her!" silently, then lifted his semi-erect penis and stroked it lustily. Jim did the same and suddenly the touches of Jo Ann's mouth began reaching May. Still bemused and rather angry, she remembered that the twins had caught her this way once before. Thinking of that she remembered how much she had enjoyed Atsuko Hachimura's attentions when they had met under similar circumstances in Tokyo. Immediately her juices began flowing again. her hands descended to the girl's blonde towel-covered head and she urged her on by thrusting her full ripe hips forward. Grateful murmurings and lickings came from under the towel. The men smiled and winked and May knew what she was going to do. They began masturbating in time to her own movements. Her eyes fixed on the two stroking hands and the precious rods they held. She pulled the towel from Jo Ann's head, notwithstanding the fear of discovery, revelling in the submission of the smooth blonde hair at her crotch.

She watched for a time, peering over her generous breasts, as Jo Ann licked and sucked. The younger woman's fingers were firmly embedded into the older woman's cunt, and May allowed herself the luxury of enjoying the service. She spread her legs wider, and her hands directed the girls knowledgeable mouth to the spots she enjoyed. Her body began reacting more strongly and she treated the blonde head more roughly, pulling it to her and rubbing herself furiously onto the willing mouth. One of her hands rose to her breast and began squeezing them furiously.

Then as her climax approached, she raised her breast to her lips and sucked on the prominent nipples.

The delight of her joint actions with Jo Ann, and the thought of the two young men spying helplessly and masturbating before her brought on May's climax. She breathed harshly, pulling Jo Ann's face to her pussy and rode herself to a climax. The closet door closed and the two young cocks hid themselves from her sight.

She raised Jo Ann to her feet. The young girl's lips, nose, and cheeks were covered with May's pungent juices. Her eyes were glazed and she was panting.

"I've never been able to do that before, all in the open like this," she smiled wanly. "I wanted to do it so much . . . Did you have to leave Omaha because of this as well?"

"No dear. I left when Henry found a job here. Do you you really like it? Shall we do some more?" May asked, stroking the slick cheeks and staring directly into the brown eyes.

"Yes, very much!"

"But you'll have to do what I say," May continued.

"Anything. Oh anything darling," Jo Ann's hands shook and she hugged May fiercely. May's breast were crushed against the cotton top and the embroidery rasped pleasingly against her stimulated breasts.

"Stay there," she ordered, slipping out of the girl's embrace. She walked gracefully over to the mussed bed, watching herself in the full length mirror on the beside the bed. She swayed her hips, conscious of the fact that Jo Ann had swivelled to watch her. She pulled back and smoothed the sheets, aware that Jo Ann was peering between her legs at her generous purse. As if unconsciously, she raised one knee onto the bed, allowing the other girl an opportunity to examine her fully. She lay back in the bed, her legs spread. One hand diddled her clitoris idly, while the other stroked a full flattened breast, pinching the nipples with care. She was aware of the hidden male eyes watching her every movement, and a flush spread out from her belly to her face.

"Strip for me," she ordered Jo Ann.

Jo Ann complied, an excited smile lighting up her face. The top went first, drawn over her head. She shook her long blonde hair free, then reached slowly for the fly of her jeans. Teasingly she worked the zipper downwards, then swayed around to show the descent of the blue fabric over her thin buttocks. She turned around again, kicked of the fabric, and slid down her panties. May admired the shape of the younger girl's body. She had a full bush of dark brown hair which she was fingering dreamily. May motioned her to approach. Jo Ann moved as if hypnotized, then she knelt between May's legs and kissed her full cunt, allowing her lips to steal into the musky interior. May stroked her head, smiling to herself. She was not too pleased at the interruption, but was ready to make use of it. A year ago the idea would not even have occurred to her. But since she had met the twins, and had allowed her imagination and preferences free reign, she found that many, though not all her inhibitions had gone, vanished under the fell of her own imagination and pleasure.

"Do you like men as well?" She whispered.

"Sometimes, but not as much," Jo Ann said raising her head from between May's legs. Her face was damp with May's discharges and she licked her lips hungrily. "They're OK, I guess. At least when I don't have a woman to love me."

"I'll love you like a man. Like two men, in fact. Go to the dresser."

Puzzled but obedient the blonde girl slipped off the bed and walked towards the dresser. She watched May's eyes on her buttocks and figure, eyes which flickered to the front sight displayed in the mirror.

"Open the bottom drawer," May commanded almost in a whisper. Jo Ann bent forward, knowing she exposed her full ass and cunt to May's gaze. Her legs were smooth and the sparse dark hair on her cunt almost invisible from the back. Her inner lips were long and stuck out beyond the outer ones, the pink contrasting prettily with the brown of her thighs and the white line inside her bikini marks. In the drawer she found a flat lacquered box. She brought it to May as ordered.

May smiled at her, kissed her lips briefly, and opened the box. "Know what these are?"

Jo Ann gulped and stared bug eyed at the two *harigata*. They had been parting gifts from Andy and Jim. Exact copies of their cocks made skillfully by a craftsman who specialized in such things in Kappabashi. They nestled in a lined box which also included a set of metal balls, several rings and other implements whose use Jo Ann could guess at, but had never seen.

May extracted the long dark shafts from the box. "I'm going to use them on you, both of them." There was a shade of cruelty in her voice. She was still annoyed at Jo Ann's intrusion into her life.

"Oh, for my ass you mean?" Jo Ann said casually.

"You've been fucked in the ass?" May said incredulously.

"The boys back home do it all the time. Practically have to put a cork in your ass if you want it any other way on a date," Jo Ann giggled. "It's nice sometimes."

"What I love are my breasts," May confided, leaning back on a soft pillow. She raised the objects in question, displaying them proudly. Jo Ann looked down at her own small pointed tits and a look of envy crossed her face for a moment, then she scooped May's breasts up in her hands and bent down to kiss each nipple.

"Love me," May breathed into her ear. "Make love to my breasts, with your mouth.

The two men stole out of the closet. Jo Ann was snuffling at May's tits, oblivious to the world, enjoying the pleasure of the sensitive fleshy mounds. Her left knee was raised, supported by May's arm as May diddled both the openings between her legs, lubricating them both with the lotion from her bedside stand. She reached for Andy's erect cock, stroking the smooth length of it, then guiding it to Jo Ann's gaping vagina. He thrust home and May's fist, guiding its entry rubbed against Jo Ann's crotch. Jo Ann tried to raise her head but was held in place by May's commanding arm. Jim, looking on bemused, was ordered around Andy. He climbed onto the bed while May squirmed and yelped to cover his approach. He straddled the girl's buttocks casually, not touching her, and May directed the tip of the cock to Jo Ann's bobbing ass. May found the tiny muscular hole, well slicked by the application of lotion, and she slipped the cock tip into it. Jo Ann squealed something into May's breast. The warm shaft disappeared slowly into her cavernous ass and Jim smiled into May's lust-glazed eyes.

"Do it," Jo Ann chanted. "Do it while I do you." Her lips returned to May's generous breasts and her fingers sought for the slick entrance to the older woman's cunt.

Taking their clue from Jo Ann's demand, the two men started fucking her with all their might. Jo Ann was not sure when she realized that the stiff erections in her were male, not rubber, but all she did was to suck harder at May's breasts. She could feel the older woman's cunt run with moisture and she applied her fingers and the palm of her hand with a will to the demanding lower mouth. May was squealing, a high pitched sound that made the two men ram firmly into Jo Ann while their hands south for May's breasts and squeezed them forcefully. Jo Ann started squealing in her turn as she felt her climax arrive from the two shafts that had been inserted in her. Her muscles spasmed and she clenched her hands over the men, digging all the sets of fingers deeply into the willing flesh. May, who was on the bottom, erupted with a powerful climax as Jo Ann jammed her fingers deep into the willing, saturated cunt. She gave a final yelp herself, feeling as if she were being torn apart with pleasure as the two men she had never seen erupted into her, flooding her interior with their juices and slicking the continues movement of their flesh into hers. Then she quivered, almost falling off May, and added her own fluids to those staining the bedsheets.

May slipped out from the bottom of the pile and watched greedily as the two cocks withdrew from the other woman's holes. The sights of cocks withdrawing from flesh other than her own had intrigued her since she had met Jim and Andy in Tokyo, and now she indulged her passion as the softening, shiny shafts slid slowly from the matted hair between Jo Anns thighs and buttocks.

Jo Ann flopped round on the massive bed and had her first look at her partners. She had thought at first that one of them might be May's husband, Harry. She would not have objected, because of the pleasure of satisfying her own lust on May. But now she saw, to her pleasure, that they were both unknown young men. She smiled at them lazily, and reached for their come-slicked cocks.

"Get them ready for me," May said watching the three young people in her bed. She bent her head and butted Jo Ann's legs aside. The girl willingly parted her legs and cried out her delight. May's tongue reached for the folds of her cunt. Her hands willingly manipulated the two cocks which soon grew hard again, ready to perform for her. She aaahed pleasurably at the feel of May's tongue as she sought out the center of her pleasure and sucked in Jo Ann's prominent clitoris. Before she could reach another climax though, May withdrew and rested on her heels on the bed. Jim and Andy looked at her expectantly. Their hands reached for her.

"Now you'll all do me," May commanded. She straddled Jim and inserted him deeply into her cunt. Jo Ann lay across Jim's chest, her mouth alternatively nipping and sucking at the softly descending bags. Andy mounted May from behind and she cried out happily as his hands came around and squeezed her breasts roughly just as his cock slid up her rectum.

"Now!" she commanded, and her willing harem set to work, leading her to paradise.

"I think we should go back to Tokyo," Andy said

thoughtfully. Jo Ann had departed on her own affairs, but May knew she would be back and willing, whenever the chance came up. They had all dressed lazily, and the two men had been talking in a low voice for some time.

"Yeah? Why?"

"First, we can't hide here forever. Second, murder is much easier here than in Tokyo. Third, Tokyo is at least our home ground, and we have a better chance there. If Mayumi has settled things with Dads, then maybe we can ask them for help as well. I don't know who that female assassin is, but I don't think we should hang around here to humor her, or any of her pals who might come along."

May hugged them to her. "Much as I would be sorry to lose you, I think I agree. I'll see you again though?" There was a slight edge of concern in her voice. She could rarely forget that they were much younger than her, and that while young girls like Jo Ann held a continuing appeal, she was already well into middle age.

As if divining the source of her worry, Jim squeezed her tit roughly and said "If you ever try to get away from us, I'll simply force you. You're definitely one of the best."

CHAPTER 16

LOVERS AND THEIR LADS

An elderly gate of greying wood hit their front door and the tiny cat's leg garden from the gaze of passers-by. Andy and Jim stepped into the tiny garden and walked across the gravel. They were home. Chieko and Mineko, both dressed in similar flower-print frocks were turning away from the door. They smiled joyfully at the two brothers and stood waiting, delightfully framed in the dark wood of the entrance. Andy felt the heart pound in his breast. He had had Mineko, but the thin intensity of Chieko now filled him with a rush of lust. He smiled into her eyes as Jim fumbled with one hand at the door, the other clasping Mineko.

Andy licked his lips once, bent to Chieko's ear and said crudely "I want to fuck you!" His mouth descended further to clamp to her neck. She shivered momentarily then stood there passively as Andy ran his hands over her figure. She was starting to fill out, she knew, and the sudden straightforward approach of this *gaijin* was testimony to the return of her pre-marital figure. The shopping expedition from Gifu was becoming precisely what she needed. Her skin burned at the touch of his hands and she longed to be out of her clothes. She wondered how similar his cock was to Jim's. Mineko had described it, as well as his preferences in detail, but there was nothing like first-hand knowledge.

He led her into the *genkan* his hand on her elbow. "I'm going to fuck you here, now," he husked. His eyes were glazed with lust and she knew that she could not resist him, could not even think of fighting his intensity. He dropped his flight bag. She squatted to the floor, leaning over onto the raised polished floor of the house platform. He fumbled behind her, lowering her hose and panties, raising her skirt over her back.

The first penetration of his cock was brisk and painful. Her own moisture had not risen. She could feel every bit of the hard cock as it forced its way into her dry canal. In some ways it was like losing her virginity to Jim again, and the mere thought of that momentous event brought down the moisture from her insides. Andy pulled her hips roughly to him. he was gasping impatiently, his cock shuttling furiously into her. She bent forward and slid a hand between her legs. The slaps of his thighs against hers resounded like gunshots, and his two nuts swung against her hand like clappers of a bell. With each shove of his hips he aahed, and he rode her like a stallion, concerned only with his own pleasure. Her hands stole to the opening of her flowery dress and she pulled at her breasts, the nipples burned in her palms and she twisted at them viciously, extracting just the right mix of painful pleasure from the engorged flesh. She raised her head slightly, and through the waves of pleasure that were washing over her managed to see Jim and Mineko. She was on her back and his muscular form was between her legs. Her heels were locked together behind his back which was curling and uncurling as the length of his cock rammed furiously into her. The mouths of the two lovers were clamped together, and both their eyes were closed. To her surprise Chieko felt no envy. To the contrary, she felt the erotic presence of Jim inside her, as his twin brother pumped at her back. She turned her head and gasped "Kiss me!" Andy's lips descended on hers and sucked at her hungrily.

Her tongue darted out and she flicked herself in and out of his cock in time to the metronomic beating of his shaft against her cervix.

His movements speeded up. Unwilling to miss the entire gamut of pleasure, she felt his balls again, then stroked the entrance to her own cunt. The lips were distended around his stem, gripping the shaft as fiercely as her mouth gripped his. Then he broke free from her mouth, gulped some air, and dove for her again. His hands became rougher, shaking her hips against his belly, pulling cruelly at her flesh. She felt as if her were penetrating to her heart and the sweet roughness brought her own climax to a pitch. She dug her nails into the floor, pushing back against him, then abandoned the floor and sought for her own tits and pussy. She drummed her fingers against her clitoris vigorously, digging one finger into herself along with his cock. The underside of his shaft jerked once, then again, and then she could feel the rush of fluid along his maleness. She cried out in a long and triumphant wail as her own fluids joined his. Her insides convulsed in a shimmering cascade of muscular tremors and her ass rammed against his immobile contracted belly muscles.

Jim watched the final throes of Andy and Chieko's love-making. There was something odd about the living room, Jim thought, but he was too wrapped up in Mineko, his hand between her buttocks, his mouth clamped to her sweet full nipple. The four of them lay at peace on the floor, the tensions and heat of the day seeping slowly away.

They stirred leisurely and Chieko became conscious of the hardness of the floor. Andy helped her up and she started to adjust her clothing. He stopped her with a gesture, then started stripping her completely. She stood in bemused silence as his hands flew over her clothing, dropping it onto the polished wooden floor of the hallway.

"While you are here, you wear nothing," he hissed menacingly.

She giggled at his intensity and the mock severity of his face broke into a smile.

"Mineko too," she whispered.

Mineko was indeed not wearing anything. When she saw Andy and Chieko approach she rose gracefully from the *tatami* and reached for her clothes. Chieko stopped her with a slight laugh. "No clothes?" she said doubtfully.

Chieko shook her head. She fell to her knees before the other girl. "You are so beautiful. All of us love you and I think we will have you now."

Mineko looked from one intense face to the other. Then she rose gracefully and bowed to them very formally. In a semi-daze she let Chieko mastermind the activities.

The pile of the carpet, laid over *tatami* in the Western-furnished section of the living room was soft and pleasant. The two men embraced Mineko's full figure, kissing her skin, tracing the lines of her legs and hips. Chieko joined them momentarily, then stood back, entranced by the vision of her friend and lover embraced by two men. Jim, standing behind Mineko stroked her full buttocks gently. His hands slipped into the crack of her ass. He had never fucked her there and suddenly and overwhelming desire to have her that way rose in his imagination. His slick cock rose against her soft flesh. As if divining his intention she leaned forward at the waist. Andy stepped forward and she bent still further, taking his slick cock into her mouth. It tasted delightfully of his sperm and Chieko's familiar flavor. She sucked the flaccid tube in, then worked her lips and tongue to bring it to a state of readiness. Chieko knelt at her side and licked at Andy's balls from below, sparing an occasional butterfly kiss at Mineko's busy face, then drifting inexorably downwards to her hanging breasts. She lingered, there, alternatively kissing each breast like a calf drinking from its mother's teat.

The feel of Mineko's full buttocks was overwhelming. Jim felt a rush of love and tenderness well into his breast. He held his stiff cock in one hand, parting her golden-colored buns with the other. The broad knob of his cock made tiny circles at her muscular rear entrance. For a second he was afraid to penetrate her. The hole seemed to tiny, too delicate for the entrance of such a large object. Then he recalled that an object of exactly the same dimensions—Andy's cock—had already penetrated the entrance with no obvious damage, and to the great obvious delight of the owner. He pushed slowly forward. One of her hands gripped his thigh, urging him in.

Jim stopped his advance once the head of his prick was inserted fully, intending to allow her time to adjust, but her urgent demands were transmitted painfully from her grip on his thigh. He sank deeply into her until his hair rubbed scratchily against the soft tissues of her backside. Pulling slightly backwards he began leisurely shafting her, rubbing his pubis against her ass in tiny little circles which brought approving pats from her hand on his side.

Chieko kissed her way lower down Mineko's soft belly. The flesh quivered gently at the delicate touch. She reached the other girl's full cunt. She knelt between the male and female legs and admired the pistoning of the man's strong cock into the willing female ass hole. The edges of the entrance gripped the shaft reluctantly as it withdrew, and fled coyly as the massive male shaft sunk deeper into the welcoming warmth. Chieko kissed her way up Mineko's smooth leg, the lapped intently at the empty cunt, inserting slim strong fingers to help her on. She was rewarded by muffled cries, joined soon by the louder cries of the men as the orgasm she set in motion translated itself to the men's cocks. She withdrew, anxious to participate herself before the men erupted.

Chieko rose from all fours. Mineko was gripping Andy's waist while she sucked lustfully at Andy's erection. Her normally full cheeks were hollowed with the effort of her sucking and Andy's eyes were closed, blissful, from her expertise.

"Help me get Jim onto his back," Chieko asked in a low voice. Andy opened his eyes, seemed ready to object, then withdrew regretfully from Mineko's welcoming mouth.

Together they slid the joined couple to the floor amidst much giggling, Jim still inserted into Mineko's ass. Jim lay comfortably on his back, his hands clasped around Mineko's full breasts. She spread her legs wide, enjoying the feel of the prick held immobile in her rectum. Andy knelt between her legs as Chieko slid several *zabuton* cushions under Jim's obliging buttocks. Mineko trembled with delight and gasped twice, first as Jim's raised hips forced his cock deeper into her distended rear, then as Andy nudged his cock and slid fully into her. Chieko admired her handiwork, then as Andy's movements began to tell on his two partners, she hurried to join in the fun. Straddling Mineko's face she set to work with her lips and tongue at the top of Mineko's cunt where the tiny clitoris was exposed by Andy's violent slammings into her interior. She was presently rewarded as she felt Mineko's velvety tongue inserted into her hungry cunt. Her buttocks were parted by strong male hands, and thick male fingers were inserted into her cunt and ass hole, while Jim nibbled at her knees and calves.

The four of them rocked together to a mighty climax. Waves of delight washed over them and their juices flooded out, threatening the carpet. The jerking of Andy's cock against her face was the first warning. He pumped his fluids into Mineko and Chieko lapped up the excess that squeezed past the pumping shaft. She felt her own juices flood her canal and they were washed away by Mineko's loving tongue, as Mineko herself felt the flood of sperm from Jim's balls fill her rear entrance.

They collapsed into a laughing happy heap, squirming with the delight of the tiny orgasms that still rippled through all of them.

Andy raised his head from Chieko's back suddenly. "Who the hell are you?" Jim heard him ask.

"Ruby," came the throaty reply.

He struggled out from under the pile and saw, with mounting horror, the face of the female assassin from the party. "Its her!" He shouted. "The assassin from LA."

CHAPTER 17

KISSING COUSINS

"That's right. I missed you there," Ruby said. Her dark handsome face bore a faint smile. Jim watched her nervously, terribly conscious of his vulnerability. He tried to move unobtrusively, but was hampered by being at the bottom of the pile of bodies. Mineko and Chieko, barely understanding the exchange, still lay as they had been before.

"There was some confusion in LA. I traced you there from Tokyo, then chased you back here. I've been waiting for you for a day. I'm glad I found you finally." The two men sat up, trying to cover themselves. "No, please, don't bother on my behalf. I like watching. I'm your cousin. Ruby Typhon, by the way. Can anyone join?" She raised her hand to her sweater and pulled it over the head. Under it she wore nothing. Her small coral-tipped breasts were magnificently firm and erect.

"At last," Jim yelped. "One of the fabled Typhons. I thought you were a hired killer. I saw you at the party . . ." He was unable to continue. Overwhelmed by relief, he started laughing weakly.

"Overactive imagination," Andy said of his brother. "Yes, you should join us?" He looked at her breasts in appreciation. She was tanned and the fine bones of her face gave her a character that shone from within. She wore a bulky sweater and slacks which did not show much of her figure, but he trusted it was as tasty as the rest of her. Her hawk-nosed face, somewhat similar to Jim's, and presumably to his own, quirked with a smile. "It'll take some time for us men to be ready of course, but if you like Chieko and Mineko . . ."

"No it won't," Jim said triumphantly. "Let me get my bag. Mayumi left me something. She didn't waste it all at Sunshine House." He padded naked into the hall, and the three women watched his firm ass retreating from them with interest. He returned with a tiny travel bottle of aftershave lotion. Andy grinned at the sight.

"Aftershave?" Ruby raised her thick eyebrows when Jim returned.

"Nope." Andy said. "SuccSex, right? I've been chasing that bloody bottle around the world, and my idiot brother had it all the time."

"Part of the time," Jim corrected. He turned to Ruby and assisted her with her slacks. The four of them looked at her curiously. She bore their examination with humor, pirouetting around to let them satisfy their curiosity. After all, it was only fair. She had seen far more of them over the past quarter of an hour.

Jim opened the bottle and dabbed some of the peach colored liquid onto his hand. He kissed Ruby and she responded ardently. He rubbed some of the liquid into her bush, then stroked her ass, her full breasts and their erect nipples, her back. A fragrance rose, flowery, unfamiliar. It enhanced her nostrils ability to detect the smell of sex, churned her insides, blew the smouldering fire of sex between her legs into a full blaze. Her cousin stood away from her and she posed there, enjoying the sensations for a long moment before doing anything to encourage it. Jim stepped back, bent over each of the Japanese girls in turn, and rubbed some more of the stuff into their matted pubic hairs, their armpits, their breast and necks. Finally he passed the tiny bottle to Andy and rubbed his hands over himself.

Ruby resisted the sight as long as she could without participating. The men were the first to respond physically. Their tired members revived suddenly, jerked to live and full tumescence. Their eyes still on Ruby, they began feeling the two Japanese women. Ruby swallowed hard. her nails dug into her palms. She wanted to scream and dive into the knot of limbs before her. But the observant part of her mind and her training held her off as a dispassionate observer. Suddenly she realized that she had smelled the scent before. In the party in LA where she had rescued Jim from the Sunlight House goons, the party that had turned into a mass orgy.

Andy grinned delightedly at Ruby's bemused face. There was a streak of exhibitionism in him which he had never admitted to, not even to Jim who shared most of his thoughts. The idea of a lovely woman watching him make love was enough to spur him on. He turned back to Chieko.

"Who is she?" Chieko whispered suspiciously.

"Our cousin," he replied truthfully to her cunt.

"Does she have to watch like that?" Chieko complained.

"Yes!" Andy said and bit her thigh viciously. "She's evaluating us for performance in the sexual olympics." Chieko subsided, the alarm she had felt because of the woman gradually gave way to the pleasure of having someone watch as she fucked. She had enjoyed that aspect of it since her first time when Jim, Nakabe, and Ito had watched and had her successively.

"Let's be more comfortable though. Jim's *futon* will hold us all."

Andy was trembling with lus as he parted Ruby's perfect legs. The mossy patch at the juncture of her legs was curly, and Chieko looked on with critical interest, feeling her own pussy. Smooth hair was so much nicer, she decided. Ruby wailed, a high-pitched ululating cry of lust and abandonment as she felt the length of Andy's shaft pierce her body. She clamped her arms and legs around him. Urging him on with blunt fingers. Their mouths sought each other's and their tongues flickered in brief loving battle. Andy's ass curved S-like as he inserted and withdrew in luistful demand. Ruby was wet throughout, but her internal muscles were well-trained and they squeezed hungrily as he penetrated. Their movements became a whirkwind of activity. Ruby's passion was uncontrolled. She cried out in a high falsetto, completely different from her normal throaty accents. Her fingers rasked into Andy's back and her thighs clamped against him in a powerful frenzy. Chieko squatted down and examined the action from behind. The European woman's asshole, darker than the pale flesh was hidden at times as Andy's full bag banged against her. When he pulled out Chieko could see a rime of white froth covering the shaft and gradually oozing over the stretched and parted lips. Then the long shaft was jammed fully into the hungry orifice. The man's buttocks moved about in a smal circle, pulled out again, then jammed deeply into the pale flesh. White sticky fluid oozed thickly from the juncture of the two bodies. The two lovers lay still.

Hardly knowing what she was doing Chieko rose to her feet. Jim and Mineko were clutching one another, though their eyes were on Ruby and Andy. Chieko tapped Andy on the back, then when he turned his head to her, motioned him off. She slipped into his place with alacrity. Ruby's eyes were still closed and she was breathing noisily. She opened her eyes to see Chieko's smooth face bending over to hers. The girls' mouths opened and they exchanged a deep soulful kiss. They explored one another's bodies lazily but thoroughly. Chieko's fingers Ruby's full breasts and she was conscious that her own smaller ones were being touched thoroughly, nibbled on, the perky dark nipples kissed with great expertise and fervour. She raised her body and explored between Ruby's thighs. The gluey mass of hairs excited her and she dipped her sharp-nailed hands between the relaxed, semen coated lips of

Ruby's warm sex. Without hurrying she rose to squat over the European girl's form. They exchanged a look of agreement. Chieko changed her position. Her head between Ruby's legs, she explored further. The smell was strange, stronger and muskier than Mineko's Overlaying the feminine muskiness was the sharp bitter tang of male essence, something she had smelled on Jim and Andy. She licked at the combined slickness at the hairy opening. The taste, far from revolting her, actually raised her lust to fever pitch. She spread Ruby's buttock and began eagerly sipping at the calyx of flesh spread out before her. Ruby responded, parting the Japanese woman's thighs and examining the slick, semen bedrenched entrance. Then she too began using her tongue.

Jim watched the two women on his *futon* for as long as he could. As they brought one another to a climax he knew he could not wait any longer. He edged forward. Mineko suddenly clutched at him fiercely. He turned to her in surprise. Her eyes were on the two women on the bedding.

"It will be my turn. When they finish," she said fiercely.

"We can both . . ."

"No!" She said, and her voice was almost a hiss. He wanted to contradict her, but her sudden desire showed a new part of her character. She had always been so meek and soft, now . . .

Mineko mounted the willing Ruby with a ferocity and abandon that surprised both of them. At first she rode the other woman like a man, rubbing her breasts and the vee of her legs against Ruby with a passionate enthusiasm. Ruby was soon gasping with the rise of another orgasm. They felt one another with abandon, Ruby taking pleasure in leading Mineko's inexperienced hands to her most intimate places. Then Mineko pulled back. She quickly laid on of Ruby's thighs over her own. Their fired pussy's were now kissing. Holding one another's shoulders they rubbed fiercely, staring into one another's eyes, kissing occasionally with deep passion and abandon. The other three moved up, entranced by the tribadic sight while Mineko and Ruby were lost in their own passion.

They approached a climax and clunf togethere fiercely. The muscles on their bellies rippled and they clutched at one another's breast uttering endearments in Japanese and English. The crisis passed and the two started moving again. Mineko caught sight of Jim's erection. She was almost out of control again. Her hand grasped at the air, then connected with Jim. She pulled him to stand between herself and Ruby. She bent the vertically standing member and aimed it at Ruby's questing lips. "Suck him, now!" Mineko said.

There was no need for translation. Jim's fierce erection was absorbed into Ruby's willing and demanding mouth. He jerked suddenly as the first of his load began emptying. Then he felt Mineko parting the valley of his behind. Her tongue slipped out and began laving the length of his slit, concentrating on his balls. Her jerked once again, then spewed a full load into Ruby's waiting throat, conscious of the tongue between his legs, aware that both women were coming to a climax as he squatted over them.

"I am afraid Mineko-chan and I must leave. We promised we would be back today. We have been in Tokyo too long."

"You will come again?" Ruby asked, almost pleaded. The three women looked at one another in understanding. The afternoon had gone very well, almost compensating the two Japanese women for the days without Jim and Andy. They kissed Ruby softly as they rose to search for their clothes. There was a promise embedded in the embrace.

"Now we must talk business," Ruby said stroking her sides and sniffing the odor of all her lovers mixed with her own. She was sorry the other two had left. There was something indefinably attractive about them both, and she herself was quite aware of the special tie between Jim and Mineko. "We have a problem that needs settling." Confronted by the reality of these two long-lost cousins of hers, she felt somewhat nervous. Family loyalty was strongly impressed into Typhon children, and she had grown up with clan loyalty considered a primary virtue. What if they did not measure up? True, as lovers they seemed more than adequate, possessing all the ancestral qualities that their genetrix had had in full measure. The wet condition of her crotch and the relaxed feeling in her body bore full testimony to that. But did they have anything else to commend them?

They lay on either side of her, not asking any questions. Facing them, she decided on honesty. "I don't imagine you know much about us, about the Typhon family, I mean. I have to admit I don't know much about you either. My cousin Leon, our cousin that is, is in charge of that part of the family business which deals in cosmetics and things. Leon is brilliant, but he is also ruthless. Some months ago I found out accidentally that he was interested in you, had in fact hired some gangsters to spy on you. Three days ago he admitted that he had done . . . something" her shoulder rose in a stylized shrug. "I didn't know what. But I was afraid for you, so I came here, to Tokyo, to warn you. I traced you to LA, and I followed. Then I saw you," she kissed Jim, "in the party at LA. Lost you, returned to Tokyo. I broke into the house—the Japanese aren't really good about locks and things, are they?—and waited for you." She smiled wickedly. "That was quite a show. I'm glad I dropped by."

Andy smiled without a word and squeezed her thigh.

"What do you want from us?" Jim asked practically.

"I think I know what Leon is after," she pointed to the tiny bottle that had contained SuccSex.

"Its not *ours,*" Andy said with some alarm.

"Perhaps. But how will you get him to believe you?"

"We could call up Dads and lay the whole thing on them." Jim said thoughtfully, tasting the idea.

'Who are Dads?"

They told her of their paternal ancestry, and she suppressed her laughter. "Now that *really* is well up to

Typhon tradition. Aunt Mary really must have been something. But seriously, telling your fathers about it would only place us, particularly me, in the middle. We are raised to be loyal to the Typhon idea.''

''Which is?''

''The family started during the days of Louis Napoleon when three siblings: a sister and two brothers, decided to try and build a mercantile family powerful enough not to be controlled by any political machine such as old Louis'. Eugenics was big at the time, and all three had children by the best partners they could find.''

''Seems to me they just enjoyed sex,'' Jim commented.

''That too,'' she agreed calmly, squeezing his soft penis. ''But there was more to it than that. They chose only the brightest children to raise as Typhons. The rest were, are I should say, given a lot of money and no power over family finances, and told to go off and play. The family corporation is pretty big, and there's more hidden—in holding companies and suchlike—than on the surface. The playboys and girls make an excellent smokescreen.''

''Sounds like a Japanese *Zaibatsu*, a family combine.''

''Quite likely,'' she said, shrugging her shoulders. The motion caused her brown breasts to jiggle delightfully, and Jim put a hand on them to still the distraction.

''Anyway, our problem is to deal with Leon first. He is in Yokohama. I have the address here.'' She procured a piece of paper. ''Its a private club of some sort. I have no idea what he is up to. Perhaps we ought to simply face him?''

''Its in Chinatown,'' Jim said, perusing the address. ''What is he doing there?''

''All I know is that he had reserved a place there. I have no idea why Chinatown, if that's where it is. Why not a hotel in Tokyo?''

''Lets go and have a look then.''

''Leon is extremely clever and extremely dangerous when annoyed,'' she warned them.

''We have one advantage,'' they assured her. ''We're playing on our home ground here.''

CHAPTER 18

SIP THE WINE, EMPTY THE FLAGON

They set the wheels in motion at once. They all felt they needed as much information as possible about Leon's intentions. The address would be a good starting point and the two brothers set out to find as much as they could about it. As usual it was a cooperative effort between Jim's ability at manipulating electronic networks and data banks and Andy's sense of where money was and what it was doing. Ruby watched quietly as they worked their way through various possibilities, Andy on the phone, Jim in front of his computers.

They correlated their information. The address in Yokohama was owned by a company, part of a large complex which owned an extraordinary amount of real estate, stocks, and other properties. For a private club it generated a huge amount of revenue. Another mystery which could only be solved on the spot.

Yokohama Chinatown was not far from the shore, and the smells of sea air washed over them as they penetrated its narrow streets, redolent with the smells of Chinese spices and incense. The address Ruby had supplied was a modest building on a small side-street. It was sandwiched between a glass-fronted modern building serving a trading company, and a run down brick warehouse which might have come straight out of the nineteenth century: Yokohama Chinatown streets tended to look like that.

They climbed cautiously up the dark narrow stairs. Smells of Chinese cooking: ginger and garlic and sesame penetrated their nostrils. The landing at the top of the stairs had three doors, one of which bore a sign saying "HEAVENLY REST TEA HOUSE" The other two were unmarked. They tried the restaurant first. Inside it was much more luxurious than outside. The walls were covered with fine red brocade with a pattern of phoenixes. Snowy white tablecloths contrasted pleasingly with the red. Three *dimsum* carts steamed complacently by the kitchen, awaiting customers orders. The place was almost empty, the rush of customers would only start later. A bored waiter looked at them then turned away.

Andy shook his head. Unlikely. They tried the other doors. One was unlocked, leading only to a tiny shop full of Chinese medicine. A wizened little man with a wispy goatee peered at them over his shoulder. He had been busy lighting some incense before a small but ornate shrine anchored to the wall. He said something in Chinese, then turned back to his devotions as they closed the door.

The third door was locked. Ruby eyed it speculatively for a moment, then grinned. She knelt before the lock. Jim looked anxiously downstairs while Andy eyed the entrance to the restaurant just as nervously. The lock snicked open and the three of them crowded inside.

They found themselves at the bottom of another flight of dingy steps. They tiptoed up. The stairs took a sudden turn to the right, widened, and were covered by a lush runner. Above was another door. Ruby paused and did her magic again. This time it took her longer, and her face was strained.

"Barely made it," she muttered to Andy. "This is a real lock!"

They found themselves in a broad corridor. Andy frowned. They had traversed the entire width of the building and were now in the abandoned-seeming warehouse.

Boarded up or not, it was obviously occupied. They passed a small window. It looked down upon a lush Chinese-style garden. An ancient wisteria bush shaded a curve-gabled gazebo. The waters of a moonpond was speckled with colored carp. The end of the corridor was closed by an unlocked door. They passed through it into an opulent anteroom. The walls were gilt and red. Several tall Ching style vases stood against the walls. Two polychrome lions guarded either side of a full moon-arch, painted red and decorated with a key motif in gold. A folding screen displaying a shadow ink painting of willows blocked the arch. They passed around the screen and started through one of the most luxurious and elaborately styled room any of them had seen. Gold and lacquer furniture predominated. Jim saw what looked like a priceless Namban scroll depicting Portuguese disporting themselves with courtesans in Nagasaki on one wall. Through other arches they could see couches and beds, all done in the same luxurious style.

"Back already Leon?" An amused cultured female voice broke into their gaping examination from one side of the room. All three of them spun around. In one of the niches, on a silk-sheeted bed lolled a beautiful young girl. She was dressed in a silk robe tied carelessly at the waist. She rose to a sitting position. Her perfect almond eyes were black against her porcelain skin. Her red lips pouted somewhat, and were moistly ready for love. She regarded them carefully for a long moment while they debated silently whether to flee or wait.

"Not Leon, but yes Leon," she said in Chinese-inflected English. "*Gwai lo* are all so alike. How curious. Sister and brothers? No. What then?"

"Cousins," Ruby said, taking command.

"Cousins?" the doll said, relaxing against a fat cushion. "Cousins. Leon had just left. Abandoned me. He is somewhat selfish, your cousin. I'm afraid we parted in a bad humor."

"I know," Ruby muttered.

"Ah. I see dissension in the family. Not good, not good at all." But still, he is a selfish man. Would you like some tea? Welcome to the Room of the Seventh Happiness." She slipped silently from the bed, stepping into tiny brocade slippers, then slipped across the floor to a low tea stand. The men watched her movement in fascination. She seemed to glide across the floor. When she returned and motioned them to sit in her alcove, they could see that she wore nothing under her robe. Pale porcelain limbs and the sight of perfect globular breasts flashed as she moved.

She looked at them solemnly, her hands cradling a cup of tea in her lap. They sipped theirs, Ruby making a face: the tea had a peculiar flavor. She wished for some sugar and the thick cream she was used to.

"He will not be back for some hours. Is there something you want of him? I assume it is clandestine, since you have no keys to this place. You are not therefore members."

"Er, . . . No. How does one become a member?" Andy queried.

She looked at him for a moment, her eyes unfathomable. "One must be recommended by a member, naturally. And of course be able to afford the charges. However, in this particular case . . . Since you are Leon's kin and since he *has* paid for much which he has not used . . . He is so . . ." she muttered something in Chinese, then drew the character on her palm.

"Uncouth?" Jim supplied.

"Yes," she said simply. "You read Chinese?" She smiled at him and the hint of thread that had been in in her voice softened somewhat. She looked at them blandly.

"A little bit," Andy said. "I can read some of the classics, but I really read only Japanese fluently."

"The classics? *Chi'ing ping Mei*? The Book of the Plain Girl?" she asked impishly.

"Something of the sort," he grinned back. "That started my interest in Chinese," he added without embarrassment.

"How wonderful. An educated *gwai lo* then."

"Tell me," Jim asked after a small sip, "What services did Elder Cousin Leon order that he did not enjoy?"

She smiled slightly, her red lips pouting even more.

"Why, Hsi-wen of course, that is to say, my own person."

"Is there anything we can do to apologize for Elder Cousin's boorishness?" Andy asked, catching on to the name as quickly as Jim. He bowed formally and introduced himself and the two others.

Though she did not understand the references, Ruby too was quick to catch on "Perhaps I should allow my two cousins to discuss it with you?"

"Of course not. You should not trouble yourself," Hsi-wen said without moving a muscle. "To the contrary. I've never fucked a Western woman." She said the last without any change in her tone or expression, then rose quickly and smoothly, dropping her robe as she did so. For a brief moment she paused before them. She had a tiny exquisitely shaped body. She reached for a hidden drawer under the bed-platform. "I think I'll have all three of you," she said, turning.

The three of them looked at her without speaking. Her skin had the pearly luminscence of a jade carving. A tracery of delicate blue veins was obvious at some points, otherwise she was a perfect, exquisite doll. Her nether lips, peeping out from between a tiny heart-shaped patch of delicate fur, were as pink as the ones on her face. They were complemented by her tiny nipples. Her hips were generous in compariosn to her body. She looked fragile, ethereal.

"Well?" she said impatiently as they examined her in silence.

The three of them hurriedly reached for their clothing, as if they were delinquent school pupils. Hsi-wen motioned them ontop the broad couch. They sat around in a circle and she examined the three of them in turn. "You are not yet ready," she said accusingly to the men, then reached for their cocks. Without moving from her seat she bent forward flexibly and aided her manual efforts with her tiny perfect mouth. She sat back to examine her handiwork, noting with approval the Ruby had her hand between her legs.

"Almost ready," Hsi-wen murmured, then uncovered the objects she had retrieved earlier from the drawer. She held up the two dragon rings for their inspection, then fitted them to the men. Jim's had been carved of ivory. A sinuous dragon reclining in a cloud circled his erection at the base. It held a small sphere in its mouth. Every detail of animal and cloud was rendered in perfect relief. The scales and other sharp edges had been smoothed by the artist, providing only smooth knobs and the rounded pearl which nestled against the back of his shaft.

Andy's ring was of ebony. The animals of thew zodiac were depicted in great detail. They were obviously engaged in a varied combination of sexual activities. The humped back of a tortoise lay against his belly, the animal's head peering upwards. Both men looked up as Hsi-wen turned to Ruby. The Chinese woman stroked Ruby's skin, lingering in the hollows of her body, exploring her breasts and vagina with faery lightness. Then her lips descended lightly onto Ruby's.

"This is for you." She produced a V-shaped *harigata*. It was bright red, carved delicately by a craftsman who had succeeded in piercing the material without weakening it. It displayed a Chinese garden, pavillions and ponds and all. Throughout, human figures engaged in erotic activities. "It must be worth a fortune!" Andy was unable to restrain the thought. He chewed at his lip.

Thinking of something else entirely, Hsi-wen reassured him "It is not cinnabar. This is rhinoceros horn dyed with a vegetable dye. I am aware of the danger. It is priceless of course. Made for a Ming Empress." Jim recalled vaguely that cinnabar, mercuric oxide, was often used by the Chinese for medicianla purposes. It is also a deadly and insiduous poison.

She turned back to Ruby and motioned her forward. Ruby rose to her knees and Hsi-wen sank one horn of the dildo into Ruby's willing flesh. The European woman's eyes closed and she breathed deeply, cupping her own breasts. Hsi-wen moved Ruby's hips in a gentle circular motion and Ruby squealed in surprise and opened her eyes. Hsi-wen smiled up at her, then guided her onto her back on the silken covers. Ruby lay back and closed her eyes, her hips rising and falling, undulating with her pleasure. A faint clinking sound came from the horn that jutted like a formidable male erection over her belly. The two men questioned the Chinese woman with their eyes.

"Two silver balls inserted into each shaft from the base," she smiled slightly. "It can be better than a man."

She swung herself over the supine brunette and lowered her generous hips until the red-dyed tower had disappeared into her flesh. For some minutes she rode the other girl, stroking her feverish flesh with her cool long-fingered hands. Ruby whimpered as if in a dream. Her brown suntanned skin contrasted with the pale Ivory of Hsi-wen's. The two men watched, their hands at their sides, their cocks erect before them. Hsi-wen rode Ruby to a quivering climax and both women clung to one another, blind to the world, ignoring the two men completely. Jim was next, and as Andy looked on in bemused silence, the tiny doll figure impaled herself onto his brother's brown cock. He watched as the ivory dragon rubbed against the smooth girl-flesh, extracting dove-like cries of encouragement from Hsi-wen. As Jim's hips began thrusting into the air, she bent forward and bit his ear lobe, then pushed a hard finger into one of his thighs near his knee. "Control yourself," she whispered. "It is not time yet!"

She mounted Nady with the same calm detachment and control. The turtle-head rubbed against her clitoris, and he could tell by the internal contractions that she had reached her final orgasm. He recalled that traditionally the Chinese lay great store in a man's ability to control his semen, and manfull restrained his rising orgasm, devoting himself instead to pleasing the delicate seeming woman above him. She came again, in a delicate lady-like fashion. Only the powerful internal contractions that squeezed his cock, and the slight fluttering of her hands betrayed her calm emotionless facial expression.

Hsi-wen rose from Andy and called for more tea. The maidservant also removed the paraphernalia, wiping each item with a smooth cloth, then laying it back in its box. Hsi-wen restrained her in almost inaudible Chinese, and the rhino-horn dildo was placed before its owner. Ruby blushed, and Hsi-wen regarded her solemnly. "Again," she mouthed laying aside her tea cup.

Ruby's cry was unrestrained as Hsi-wen's skilled fingers inserted the *harigata*. Hsi-wen mounted her again, and the two women's lips joined as their hips undulated together. Then the Chinese women turned to the men. She ordered Andy around behind her and pulled apart her pale buttocks. For a moment he stared, speechstruck at the tiny dark opening that beckoned to him. It was tightly clenched, but somehow he knew it would accomodate him without difficulty. Below the entrance reserved for him he could see the bright red of the dildo emerging from the almost hairless cunt and disappearing into Ruby's beneath. Ruby's blunt-fingered hand was gently tickling the juncture of the two female bodies. Andy edged forward.

Jim crouched over Ruby's head. Her eyes were closed, but her mouth was open and her tongue licked out, greeting his balls with the fervour of long lost relatives meeting at last. Hsi-wen rounded her lips and sucked the plum-tip of his cock into her. Her pale cheeks hollowed and Jim felt his entire essence being sucked out of him. He pushed forward slowly, watching as Andy, his eyes almost closed, did the same from the other direction.

Between them Hsi-wen rested. Content. She had prepared the stage, now let her pleasure begin.

"I have tried to recreate the elegance of the houses of pleasure of yesteryear. We have some branches, in Taipei, Nagasaki, Hong Kong, and now we are considering expansion to the West. We of course are also intending to reintroduce the willow game in its proper form to Mainland China. Those bloody communists. I do not usually attend to members myself, you must realize. It is merely that we have some interest in expanding to Europe, and we had been told that Leon Typhon would be a good person to approach for a business arrangement. But he is so . . . boorish.'' Hsi-wen was speaking, her delicate form surrounded by the other three. The smell of their sex was still in the air, not withstanding the warm towels that had wiped away most physical signs. While the other lay exhausted, she showed no effects of their efforts.

''Bad for business eh?'' Andy sympathized.

''Its not that. I can do without the business. But people such as himself have ruined appreciation for so many fine things, including properly performed pleasure.''

The memory of Amsterdam and its sterile houses, of Trudy displaying herself in a red-lit window, occurred forcefully to Andy. ''Were you thinking of some place such as Amsterdam?''

''Perhaps,'' she said.

''You know,'' Andy said thoughtfully relaxing on the cushions and talking softly, as if to himself ''I bet that would be a real change. Something exotic, we could make a fortune. The ultimate business.'' He looked at Jim ''Just think how well it would fit in with Dads.''

Hsi-wen looked on, her face placid though she was aware that a new path was opening up before her.

Ruby laughed. ''Amsterdam, better watch out,'' she said. Andy agreed. The commercial sex of that lovely city could do with some oriental gentility.

''You are the sole owner?'' Andy asked, intrigued by the commercial possibilities.

''No. Merely one of the major ones. And chair of the board. And one of the star workers, of course.'' She stroked his sweaty back.

He looked at her. ''I've got one hell of a proposition for you. And a product that will . . .''

''Hey, hey,'' Jim said, divining his brothers intentions. ''First we got to make peace with Dads, and also, get out of this mess with Leon.''

''No problem,'' Hsi-wen said. ''I will take care of Leon. I admit I much prefer you three to him.''

She rang a tiny gong and another maid entered, dressed in jeans and T-shirt. Hsi-wen said something sharply in Chinese, and the other woman, after a startled glance in their direction vanished.

''It is off-hours and the staff are not yet ready to receive visitors, still, there is no excuse . . .'' she said softly.

The girl reappeared. Somehow she had managed to slip into a proper, loose Chinese robe and pin up her hair. She bowed and deposited a tray laden with brazier, cups,and a kettle of wine before them.

Hsi-wen poured the golden steaming liquid into the delicate porcelain.

''To a fruitful and lasting relationship,'' she toasted them.

''To business,'' Andy offered.

''To us,'' Ruby sipped at the fiery liquor.

''To fun,'' Jim echoed.

The three naked bodies stirred tiredly on the wide *futon*. Jim's room had no bed. Through one open sliding door his study, filled with various computer components, looked out into a tiny garden. On one wall hung a beautifully executed scroll, its purple hues dominating the room. Male and female clothes were scattered about. Jim blearing opened his eye and closed it rapidly. Even the diffuse light coming through the paper *shoji* windows stabbed his eyeballs with pain.

It took the three of them an hour to get through a lazy bath and a no less lazy breakfast. Ruby looked at Andy's raw egg, rice and soup with horror, and contented herself with toast and other items from the hefty European breakfast Jim had prepared.

"How can you eat that stuff for breakfast?" she asked, genuinely curious.

Andy stared at her in perplexity. "Its wonderful. Surely much better than a cup of coffee and slab of bread the French mistakenly call a breakfast."

She laughed "I have to agree with you there."

They held a council of war, the upshot of which was that until and unless Hsi-wen or some other source came up with information about Leon's doings, they would just have to wait. They spent the rest of the day getting more properly acquainted.

As the sun dipped colorfully below the skyline, they sipped beers and finally worked up their courage to call Clouds and Rain in Gifu prefecture.

"I'm terribly sorry about the misunderstanding, boys," 'Kitty' Kitamura's voice was subdued. "We really should not have been so suspicious of you, but . . ."

Andy managed a laugh. "Don't worry Kitty, we understand. And part of the problem was our own. We really panicked, to excess as it turned out. We do have a problem, and a business proposition for you. I can't go into details, but it relates to your attempts to revive the martial art we talked about . . ."

Several months before they had all witnessed an impressive display of a traditional esoteric martial art Fine and Kitamura were trying to resurrect. It was based on incapacitating an opponent by channeling his aggressive forces into sexual ones. Many of Clouds and Rain's employees were trained in the art. It was also related to Fine and Kitamura's enduring interest in sexual relations which had brought them to the development of the SP 15 human pheromone, the basis of the SuccSex perfume.

"If there's anything we can do to help you boys, we will." Fine broke into his partners reply. "Anyway, Mayumi should be arriving soon with a token of our apologies."

There was a sound from the entrance hall. "She's here already," Andy said into the phone. We'll talk to you later.'' He hung up and turned around, a large smile on his face.

His jaw dropped. Instead of Mayumi's beautiful face, he saw the face of two stern-faced strangers. He turned to warn his companions when he heard them cry out. Two other silent intruders had emerged from either side of their house. They were trapped.

''I sort of thought I'd find you here,'' a lazy, cultured voice intruded.

''Leon!'' Ruby looked furiously at her cousin. The twins turned to face him.

He had almost classically handsome features marred only by the large eagle-beak nose that was almost a Typhon trademark. His brown hair was carefully brushed and he wore a perfectly fitted three piece suit. His assistants stared at the three before them impassively.

''Cousin Leon!'' Jim said jocularly. The jest was hollow. Somehow it did not seem that Leon Typhon was ready to acknowledge family ties at this late date.

''How the hell did you get in here?'' Andy asked, still in shock. He couldn't muster Jim's humor at times like this.

''Aunt Mary's twin bastards,'' Leon Typhon said poisonously. ''And my dear cousin Ruby.''

''Don't do anything you'll regret Leon. The family council will hear of this,'' she said sharply.

''Not until its all over,'' he said mildly. The twins looked uneasily at one another.

''Let me explain,'' Leon said dropping negligently into Jim's favorite armchair. ''I am in charge of Typhon Enterprises cosmetics division. For some years I have been opposed in some of my markets by a major Japanese fragrances house. Now, the Japanese have taken over many branches of manufacture, and are very good at them, I'll be the first to acknowledge that. But perfumes? What do they understand in perfumes?'' He clicked his manicured nails together sharply ''Nothing!''

Jim and Andy looked on in fascination.

"I do understand that they have now developed a substance which may, I emphasize *may* be a threat to my own business plans. I intend to get their secret. *You* are going to help me."

"Never!"

"Us? Hell, we don't know what you're talking about . . ."

"I know, and you know that my previous agent, a certain Mr. Akebono was made a fool of. I've traced your movements, Mr. Middler, you see. I also know of the computer tape he so foolishly lefty in the possession of the courier I imagine that it had some manufacturing processes on it, no?" he grinned triumphantly. "These gentlemen with me are a trifle more reliable than Mr. Akebono. I'm sure they'll be able to convince you . . ."

One of the Japanese musclemen moved slightly and a faint look of speculative interest came into his eyes.

Jim, more aggressive than Andy, was about to say "Go to hell," when the doorbell rang.

Leon thought for a moment while the twin's stole tense and worried glances at one another.

"Go and answer the door," he told Ruby. "Hashimoto will accompany you. Just say that these two are absent or busy, send whoever it is away. No tricks mind. Sugiura will see to it that these dear cousins stay put. They'll also be hostages to your good behavior."

Ruby's full lips thinned to a narrow line and she walked out of the large living room to the hallway. Hashimoto, the larger of the two men in the room followed her silently. They could not hear the words, but the twins' heartbeat almost stopped. The voice was Mayumi's. The murmur of voices went on for some time, then the door was firmly closed. Ruby, with Hashimoto treading soundlessly at her heels, returned to the prisoners. The two men who had been in the garden entered as well.

"Well, I believe we are ready to begin," Leon Typhon said with relish. Andy and Jim looked from side to side for an escape as the goons closed in on them from either side.

CHAPTER 19

BLOW THAT BUGLE, THE CAPTAIN SAID

Mayumi turned away from the house with some puzzlement. Her instructions were very specific. President Kitamura and Vice-President Fine had been extremely embarrassed by their assumption of their sons' wrongdoing. So had she, since it was her actions that had turned the light of suspicion on the two brothers. She had insisted that it should be her who would convey their joint apologies. Finally Kitamura and Fine had given in. A pretty girl offering herself in apology was much more effective than two older men. She had flown to Haneda Domestic airport, then headed at top speed for Aoyama, only to find a *gaijin* girl insisting rather nervously that Jim and Andy were out. Which could not possibly be right. She knew Kitamura *sacho* would report her expected arrival time to the twins.

Rubbing her finger in perplexity she turned away from the twins gate and walked into a solid figure who had just stepped through the gate.

''Excuse me,'' she said automatically in Japanese.

''That's ok, honey,'' the black woman replied in English. ''Do you know if Mr. Suzuki and Mr. Middler live here?'' The woman's Japanese was atrocious.

''Yes, but I've been told they're not here.'' Mayumi

said in English. She looked at the other. She was an extremely handsome woman with an erect carriage and full bosom. She was dressed casually, and large gold hoop earrings glinted against her dark skin. She looked at the house, and her expression was worried. "Why do I have an uncomfortable feeling about this?"

"You are a friend of theirs?" Mayumi asked.

"Yes. They asked me a few days ago about . . . a problem." the black woman closed her mouth as if she felt she had said too much.

"Perhaps we should talk," Mayumi said. "There *is* something funny here. My employers said they would call for me. I should be expected."

The other woman looked as her without replying, then she asked "Who answered the door?"

"A ga . . . foreign woman. She was familiar somehow . . ." Suddenly her eyes widened and she said anxiously "We must do something! I remember where I saw her face before. It was in LA several days ago. Jimmu told me he was being hunted by a murderer," she gulped in fright, turned and was about to run for the door of the house and demand admittance.

"Hold on honey. You can't go in there alone, and we certainly don't know. Lets look around first."

Mayumi shook her head desperately. "No. There is something wrong, I know it."

"Lets sneak round the back first," the other suggested. "I'm Sissy McLane, by the way."

"Hajimemashite. My name is Asahi Mayumi. Now let us . . ."

Sissy stopped her. "Look kid, I can handle myself, but I don't know about you. I'll sneak around the house and sort of peek in the windows. Why don't you wait here. If there's a ruckus or I call, you hunt up the cops."

"Cops?" Mayumi was puzzled.

"Police. *polico*," Sissy said. The vernacular for police was one of the few Japanese words she knew. Before Mayumi could delay her any longer, she had walked lightly through the garden and around the house, peering through the lighted windows as she did so. In the dark she could not have been noticed by the occupants staring out into the night.

The house was built in traditional style, with a broad *engawa* veranda around three sides. The paper covered *shoji* sliding doors were closed and she could not peer beyond the external glass. The light shone through the paper cast a soft glow on the polished *engawa* floor. She rounded a corner into the back and found herself in a small formal Japanese garden. The external glass sliding doors of the *engawa* were open at one point. A murmur of voices came from the opening. Then a yell of fright. Definitely male. A female voice. Rapid swearing from someone she identified as Andy.

Sissy took a small breath to calm her stomach. This was not the first time she had entered a room held by hostiles. Her job in Counterintelligence required it, not often, it was true, but she kept herself in readiness in any case. She stooped and scooped at the gravel pathway under the eaves, then charged into the room. Her trained eye took in the sight at a glance. Two men were standing with their back to her. They were holding two struggling figures, one female, the other a male she identified as Andy, in professional armlocks. Jim was facing her. He was seated in an armchair. His hands held behind him and his face was pale and bloodless. A Japanese man was holding his arms behind him while another held a long needle in front of his eyes. A European man in a suit was leaning negligently on a *shinai*, a bamboo practice sword. He was saying something in an irritatingly smooth voice to Andy as Sissy charged into the room.

She screamed to attract their attention, and then she moved with blinding speed. Her clenched left fist hit the back of one neck while her right leg went high in a sickle kick to the the unprotected head. Both men collapsed. One held on to Andy, the other turned as he fell. There was a snap as the girl he was holding broke his arm expertly as she twisted out of his grasp. Sissy was too busy to notice the fallen targets. Her left hand continued its swing and she threw a handful of gravel and dust at the man who was holding Jim's arm. The needle-holder turned with a scowl. Seeing Sissy he slipped a hand into his jacket and drew the traditional fighting weapon of the Japanese criminal, a hand-length single edged *tanto* blade.

Suddenly there was movement from the other side of the room. Mayumi slipped in. Her dress had been tucked up into her panties and her shoes were off. She moved with the smooth deceptive ease of a trained fighter. Sissy spared her an approving glance as she prepared herself for the knife welders attack. The bamboo wielding European had dropped his ineffective weapon and his hand was streaking for his pocket. Sissy knew he was reaching for a gun, but his eyes were on Mayumi who was closer, and she did not have time to spare for him either.

The *yakuza* facing her twitched his knife hand to his left hip. The knife, facing forward and braced by the left hand was impossible to deal with using normal unarmed combat techniques. Sissy slipped aside as he passed. Unexpectedly she slipped to his left. He had been expecting her to avoid his charge, and his short slash to the right would have cut her belly open. Instead he found her on his left. His hand was seized, twisted behind his back and her hard fist slammed him into unconsciousness. Sissy turned to help Mayumi against the man with the gun. He had pulled something shining out of his pocket. Sissy screamed again. He turned in surprise. Mayumi was sliding under the blows of the last *yakuza*, and his blows lost their focus. Instead he fell to the floor, jerking uncontrollably. The European aimed a silvery tube at Sissy. He hesitated a minute, and then Mayumi was upon him. Sissy, reaching to her assistance pulled up sharply. The slim Japanese girl's hands were stroking the mans torso. He tried to fend her off, but even as he did so, his movements became uncoordinated. His hips started jerking uncontrollably and his eyes rolled back in his head. He clutched at the air, mewling as he collapsed. To her intense surprise she saw that an enormous erection was bulging the front of his pants. The tear-gas pen dropped from his hand.

Jim and Andy were grinning in relief. A therapeutic glass of ingle malt whiskey was clutched in Jim's hand. They considered the pile of bodies, unconscious, conscious, and partalyzed with desire.

"What do we do with them?" Both men were clearly out of their depth.

"He's overstepped himself this time," Ruby said dryly. She was reading the documents that they had found in Leon's pocket. "He was trying to get you to sign Mary's shares in the family company over to him. That would have made him the prince-in-waiting and a senior partner all in one."

"What about these guys?" Sissy asked more practically. The *yakuza* were all quite still, except for the one dealt with by Mayumi. He seemed in the throes of an intense erotic dream. As was Leon. Sissy wondered what the slim Japanese girl had done to them. Whatever it was, it was both nonlethal and extremely effective.

Andy too was fascinated by the two moving men. "Tell me, Ruby, what does your family, our family I should say, think of homosexuality?"

Ruby raised her heavy eyebrows in astonishment. "Private preferences are no one's business, so long as one provided an heir. In a word, they couldn't care less."

"The *yakuza* do," Jim said. He was grinning faintly. He thought he could divine his brother's mind. "Where's the instant camera?"

Leon Typhon opened his eyes to find several pairs of eyes upon him. He was slightly chilled. And he glanced down to find himself naked. His hired brawn were nowhere to be seen. In point of fact they were lying in a neat pile outside the front door. Sissy stood over them with a stick. None had stirred as yet.

"You've been very naughty, Cousin Leon," Jim leered

at him. He had a score to settle with Leon, and he intended to extract the most out of the situation.

Leon gritted his teeth. He didn't know how two women had managed to reversed the tables so thoroughly, but he had no choice but to wait patiently. "All in the line of business," he said urbanely and shrugged.

"Homosexuality? In the line of business?" Jim asked.

"What the hell are you talking about?" Leon was suddenly conscious of the extremely sexy dream he had been having.

"Why, this," Jim said and displayed some pictures. They showed Leon and his hired thug. Both were naked, both alternated in different positions. And from the state of their anatomy and the ecstatic look on their faces, it was clear what they had been up to. His eyes opened in outrage. He didn't . . . he couldn't . . .

"Repeat after me," Andy leaned over "Mustn't screw the help. Mustn't screw the help."

"It won't do you an ounce of good. The family doesn't care. Ask Ruby. The worst that will happen will be some personal social embarrassment."

"Oh, more than that. Much much more," Jim grinned. "First of course, we'll give these pictures excellent billing. To all your business acquaintances. Quite a few of them *would* care. But more important is your, . . . what shall I call him? Your paramour. The fellows you hired are *extremely* concerned about their honor. And he knows *he* was unconscious. We'll make sure he and his family know that you took advantage of him while he slept. Tsk tsk. The *yakuza* are *so* unforgiving. I doubt you'd live out the year."

Leon looked at the brothers and their cousin poisonously. Unlike the previous occasion when he had hired Japanese thugs, he had taken the trouble this time to study their habits and customs. Unfortunately, everything Jim had said was true. And in his heart he knew he was beaten. His shoulders slumped.

"What do you want then?"

''Nothing,'' they chorused to his surprise. ''Just leave us alone.''

''You see,'' Andy continued for both of them. ''Ruby says you are after all an excellent business manager in your own way. Wouldn't want to jeopardize our interest, would we? I imagine our stocks in the family business are worth more than a bit. And there's no chance we'll sign them over to you. Thanks for telling us about or dear departed mother's share. We didn't know there was such a treasure waiting for us.'' Andy grinned happily. There were few things he liked more than manipulating some valuable financial properties. He and Jim were now very rich, thanks to Leon's cupidity. ''As for your struggle with our Dads, frankly, we don't care. Its your problem, and theirs. Frankly, we think you'll lose. In any case, we are going into business for ourselves. We've been made an interesting proposition, one made to you, even if you don't know it. We accepted in your stead.'' The idea of going into business with Hsi-wen was still uppermost in Andy's mind. The possibilities were enormous. The twins rose.

''Get out of here. If you bother us again, there'll be trouble.'' Jim said threateningly. he had to control his laughter. A mocking self image came to mind. A rabbit threatening a fox. Oh well, Leon was not to know that he and Andy were both committed cowards.

Still dazed, Leon rose to his feet. His henchmen rose from the floor as he appeared. They walked out of the house together and were swallowed by the night.

Steering carefully, Millicent managed to avoid spilling her tray as she avoided the customer's groping hands. This was the third time this particular customer had come to the bar since she had started working there, and she was already able to predict his moves. She stood before the table, bowed as deeply and as gracefully as she could, and unloaded the drinks and the bill. The patrons were paying no attention to the price, paying it automatically, which was just as well because the overpriced drinks she served were not worth the money they spent. One of the men had his eyes on her shirt. The scalloped neck blouse was open and Millicent knew that her boobs were practically falling out. The other young businessman had his eyes glued to the floor under her feet. He was breathing hoarsely and his hands were clutching at the tablecloth. The mirror under her feet was slick, and in the first day she had worked the *nopan* bar she had had to be extremely cautious about her footing. She hoped neither of them were grabbers, and to reward them, she stayed as she was a tiny bit longer. Not wearing underclothes had been uncomfortable for the first few days, but she was now so used to it she actually found them uncomfortable. She allowed the man a final look at her furry slit, then turned and walked away. They sipped at their drinks, their hands trembling.

The two other girls working at the *nopan* bar were both Japanese, and though well-endowed, one even more so than Millicent, received far less attention. She smiled mechanically at Yoshio, the bar owner. He had been ready to offer her an additional source of income, but so far she had remained celibate. The truth was that she enjoyed exposing herself, and while none of the patrons had mentioned it, let alone complained, her pussy was obviously wet by the end of her working night.

The problem was of course the grabbers. Most of them were drunk and thus easily avoided, but occasionally they caught. She remembered one very painful incident in which a strong man had managed to actually hook his finger into her cunt. Yoshio had started for the man at once, but Millicent had taken an earlier hint from Sua who had been working at the bar longer. The impetuous patron had screamed and withdrawn his hand while Millicent had smiled and repinned the broach to the sash at her waist.

She was stumbling heavily by the time eleven rolled around. The place was emptying as the salary men rushed to catch the last train to whatever tiny apartment they called home. Some, she knew, had a good two hour ride ahead of them. She hoped the memory of her would keep them warm. Maybe make their wives happy. Suddenly she felt very lonely. She put her coat on and bid the others good night. The one good point about the bar was that for high pay she had to work fairly little. Nonetheless, four hours on her feet were exhausting.

She hesitated a minute, then walked to the yellow phone in the lobby. This time she hesitated for much longer, then dialed Nagoya. There was no answer from Kaoru's house and Millicent felt tears rise in her eyes. Her tiny one room apartment was so grey and unenticing. She pressed her palm, against the bulge of her mound. A thrill of desire shot through her, and she wondered if she shouldn't take Yoshio up on his offer. Then another possibility occurred to her, and she dialed again.

"Yes?" a familiar voice answered.

"This is Millicent," she was glad it was Andy: Jim's intensity frightened her somewhat. "Could I come and see you?"

"Ah . . ." There was some doubt in his voice and she thought she could hear other voices in the background. Then suddenly his voice lightened and she fancied she could see his sudden infectious grin. "Sure, why not? In fact, please do come. We've moved to another address, but its right nearby the old place. Here's the address. How soon are you going to be here?"

"Very soon," she said, hanging up after getting the address. Now to get a taxi.

"Were going to have a guest," Andy said to the room around him. Sissy stirred slightly. "I hope its another man."

Andy grinned. "Nope, sorry. A woman. A missionary."

"What?" the Black woman sat up, spilling Mayumi's head from her lap. "What the hell we need a missionary for?"

"She's going to preach at you," Jim said lazily. In his present mood he was content to deal with anything, even Millicent's preaching.

Andy grinned. There was a spark of mischief on his face. "That's right. She'll preach. Very closely too."

Jim laughed and the women looked at him without comprehension.

The doorbell rang.

"That couldn't be her," Andy said. His face paled. Jim chewed his lips nervously.

"Let's go and see," Sissy said, grabbing some clothes.

A young man was standing diffidently before the door. He wore a neat suit, and his hands were clasped nervously.

"Yes?" Andy said tiredly to him. Sissy, wearing a short *happi* coat which did nothing to hide her charms stood threateningly in the background.

"My name is Yanagisato Kaoru. I am looking for a friend of mine, Miricento Purdue." He looked so hangdog that it took Andy a moment to identify the young bus driver. Suddenly he smiled, realizing finally that that life was returning to normal. The desire to share his happiness overwhelmed him. "Come in. I'm sure we'll find her for you." He was laughing loudly as he introduced Kaoru to the group.

The young man's eyes bulged out. None of the others had had time to dress, and Andy grinned proudly at them. Jim's fingers were inserted in Mayumi's slit and he was slowly kissing Ruby's buttocks. Mayumi was stroking Ruby's soft brown hair, and Ruby herself was dozing off, exhausted by the evening's events.

Sissy came up and pressed herself against Kaoru's broad back. "Fresh meat, girls," she whispered. Her hands wound around his paralyzed chest and she began unbuttoning his shirt. At first he blushed, and then his trembling stopped and he stood there quietly as Sissy undressed him. Mayumi rose to help. Unzipping his fly she let his pants fall and reached for his starting erection. She sucked the thickening flesh into her mouth, nibbling delicately at the underside of the shaft, then licking it in apology. It stiffened miraculously as Kaoru stepped out of his pants and stood before them gloriously naked. Sissy ran her palms over his broad shoulders. She liked muscular men, and his smooth skin and regular features made him even more attractive.

Kaoru was conscious of the female hands on his skin. Then Sissy's form glued itself to his and he felt her strong hands roving between their bodies. He was conscious of her full breasts pushed against his back, then of her fur tickling his buttocks. Suddenly her hands were there, digging gently but irresistably into the muscles of his ass and hips. The other girl, the Japanese, rose, sliding her body along his until her lips could reach his chin and his mouth. Unlike the Black woman, she was shorter than he, and he had to bend slightly to reach her mouth. They kissed deeply, and then the two women grasped his shoulders and turned him around. Sissy's demanding mouth descended onto his and she explored his mouth with her tongue, while Mayumi glued her form to his back.

Jim and Andy watched with bemused appreciation as the bus driver, sandwiched between the two women, was led into the room. Sissy raised her muscular dark leg and Mayumi supported the black woman's foot with one hand, while she steered Kaoru's stiff cock with the other. Sissy raised herself on the toes of her foot, and Mayumi guided the stiff cock into the pink entrance. Sissy grinned, her teeth flashing in her brown face, as she descended slowly onto the waiting shaft. She clutched Kaoru hungrily, jerking her hips into him. He stood for a moment, resisting the pressure, then suddenly felt himself falling. The trio toppled to the ground, Sissy on top. She began wildly riding the man, her hips rising and descending with a frenzy while her fingers dug into the muscles of his shoulders and chest. Kaoru was breathing in gasps now, thrusting his hips as high into the air as he could, clutching at her anatomy while Mayumi wriggled out from under them and turned to watch. Sissy's head was raised back and the tendons in her neck were standing out. Her full breasts bobbed over Kaoru's face and he was snapping at them, trying to capture the delicate black morsels of her nipples.

Mayumi trapped one of the wildly gyrating fruit and sucked it, then fed it into Kaoru's mouth. His eyes were open yet unable to see. Ruby rose from her doze and slithered around to watch the action from behind. She could see the shaft appearing then disappearing into the delicate lips. Kaoru's hairy balls were contracting rhythmically, then swelling, and she found the sight so compelling she dipped her face forward and kissed the sac delicately. Sissy's nether hole was before her eyes and she examined it, trying to be objective. Was it indeed so sexy? As pretty as her own? She had noticed that Andy particularly enjoyed that entrance, and she had enjoyed having him in her ass as well: But all in all she preferred her vagina to be full than her rectum.

Jim and Andy watched the show for as long as they could. Sissy was soon crying wildly over Kaoru's supine form, her hair flying, as she reached another orgasm. Kaoru was obviously ready to follow, even precede her, but Mayumi's knowledgeable hands had slipped over his belly and struck where they would do the most good. Sissy reluctantly abandoned her seat and Mayumi hurriedly swung her legs over the handsome bus driver's hips. She was much gentler and softer than Sissy had been, yet her cunt was more muscular and better disciplined. Kaoru resumed his frantic bucking, dislodging her from time to time but immediately recovering. She rewarded particularly strong thrust, with her lips and hands on his face and chest and with approving squeezes of her vaginal muscles. Andy thought the man appeared actually in pain, a desperate lust settling over his body. Mayumi, fully in control, brought him to the verge of orgasm, then calmed his feverish flesh down. She repeated it again and again, never allowing Kaoru to come, approaching closer and closer to her own climax until she overtook him with a series of shudders that racked her slim body. Still she kept hold of the base of Kaoru's stick while she rose from his arching body. His cock was shiny with her juices, and his own white sperm oozed from the tip, but it was obvious she had controlled the flow.

Andy's prick was surging erect. Sissy rose lazily to one elbow, then ordered him peremptorily down. She licked the underside of his cock while holding up the precious balls with one hand. Gradually the tired member revived fully. For a moment she regretted that men had so little staying power, and that there were not more around, but then she bent to her task with greater fervor and was rewarded by seeing his flag stiffen again over his belly.

Ruby had replaced Mayumi with alacrity. The stiff cock slid into her and she gasped at the insertion. Her hands twiddled the upper entrance to her slit, exciting herself still more. She knew her own body better than anyone, and was intent on receiving as much pleasure from this stranger as she could. She looked around her, and found that she was no longer alone with the man. She laughed happily, since she enjoyed being watched, then raised her small shapely breasts proudly, offering them to any of her lovers who cared to accept the gift.

Jim was crouching behind her. "Think you can take both of us in?" he whispered.

She turned her head and kissed him "Yes," she whispered back.

His hands slid down her tanned back, lingering in the hollows and pressing into the muscles that bunched and moved under her smooth skin as she rode Kaoru. His hands parted her buttocks, fingering the tiny puckered hole at the base of her spine, moving further down to where the warm marble pillar of Kaoru's erection was tantalizing her cunt. Jim could feel the lips grasping the male teat hungrily, releasing it reluctantly as Ruby moved upwards. Jim transferred some of the fluids from between her legs to the muscular starfish hole, then knelt between their thighs and gradually began inserting himself.

Ruby bent her head as she felt Jim'slick erection penetrate the muscles of her behind. Andy rose from Sissy's grasp and stood before Ruby. Greedily she gulped at the offered cock sucking it in as deeply as she could. She laughed happily to herself. This was the first time she had ever had three men at once. Mayumi reached up a hand and started squeezing Ruby's breasts, then not content with the action, she pushed Andy aside and straddled Kaoru's face.

Mayumi's knowledge of anatomy had brought Kaoru down from a pitch of excitement that threatened constant eruption. He was dreamily contemplating the sensations and sights around him. The pressure of something against his cock had been confirmed when he saw Jim's face peering over the woman who was riding him. He felt the junction of their bodies and was not surprised to find that the other man was inserted fully into the same woman. Their shafts were separated by a thin warm wall of womanflesh. Then his sight was cut off as golden thighs surrounded him. He knew what was wanted and his lips and tongue went to work along with his hands, exploring the deeper recesses of the warm sweet flower that blocked off all sight. He stiffened his tongue and rove his fingers deeply into the tantalizing depths.

Sissy rose abruptly from the carpet. She hunted around until she could find a padded stool that fitted what she had in mind. She placed the stool behind Andy whose cock was jutting into Mayumi's greedy mouth. His eyes were closed and his hips jutted forward. Sissy forced him down onto the stool. She examined his erection critically, then bestowed a quick kiss. Spreading her legs and facing Mayumi. She straddled the man and inserted him into her hungry cunt. Mayumi smiled up at her, and then the cheerful face disappeared as the Japanese girl licked the length of Sissy's slit, alternating between the prominent clitoris, engorged by lust, and the male pole that shuttled deeply into the black girl's interior. Mayumi was conscious of fingers: Ruby's, Jim's, the drivers, she neither knew or care, stroking and penetrating her cunt and rectum. She busied herself urgently about pleasing Sissy, pleasing the others, pleasing herself.

Mayumi's unobtrusive control of the group proved itself as they built quickly towards a joint climax. When it came, the entire structure of flesh and lust quivered together. They called out, vanishing together into a squirming uncontrolled tangle of lust that shook the house boards. Kaoru could feel Jim's cock emitting a powerful jerk that pressed against his own shaft. Ruby cried out, her eyes closed and drove her tongue deeply into Mayumi's musky interior. Kaoru responded to the clutching of Ruby's muscles with a muffled cry that sent shivers through Mayumi. His long suppressed climax exploded into Ruby's channel, flooding the interior and streaming out to join the juices emitted by Jim in her rear. A large frothy pool stained the juncture of three pairs of legs and dripped down below them. Sissy found herself nearing another climax. She thrust herself deeply down onto Andy and was rewarded by the jerking signs of his eruption. She allowed herself to contract into her own pleasure as a final touch of Mayumi's knowledgeable tongue sent her int a frenzy which ground her ass onto Andy's lap.

Kaoru's cry had brought the first, quiet orgasm to Mayumi. The sight of Sissy writhing mindlessly on her tongue and Andy's prick completed her pleasure and she allowed herself to sink quietly into a racking orgasm that was enhanced as Kaoru and Ruby drove their tongues and fingers into her waiting delicate cunt.

The tremors and clutchings subsided into quiet nibbles and slow tired caresses. Unwilling to end the pleasure, they nonetheless gradually sorted themselves out, lying in a tangle of limbs and panting bodies. They were gradually drifting off to sleep, when the doorbell rang.

"Not another!" Jim said tiredly. The others laughed, though Andy rose to his feet with a grin.

"This one is special," he said. "I'll get it."

Millicent was standing at the door. Andy gaped, barely recognizing her. She was heavily made up: bright red on her lips, pink on her cheeks, and her eyes had been heavily shadowed. Her rather dull blonde hair had been washed and piled high on her head. She wore high heeled shoes with no stockings, and a thin summer raincoat.

"May I come in?" she asked. Her hands were stretched out, almost beseeching.

"Of course you may," he said. "What have you been up to?"

She smiled tiredly, then tears started running down her cheeks as she stepped up into the house. Andy held her warmly and her sobs gradually stopped. She stood away from him. Her mascara had run, but most of her makeup was intact. She dropped her raincoat and stood before him. Andy admired her at arms length. The tight miniskirt barely passed the line of her crotch. The deep-necked peasant blouse was almost transparent, and showed her bra-less breasts leaving little to the imagination. Unable to control his hands, Andy tweaked the nipples, which immediately stiffened under his fingers.

"What have you been doing with yourself?" he asked again. She hesitated for a moment, then blurted "Working in a *nopan* bar."

Andy stared at her incredulously for a moment, then hurried her to the living room. "I have an announcement to make," he called out proudly. His hands were between the cheeks of Millicent's ass. She was staring down in shock at Kaoru, who was peering up at her and trying to extricate himself from the pile of bodies.

"This is Millicent Purdue, waitress at a *nopan*."

"What's that?" Ruby whispered.

Jim laughed delightedly "*Nopan*. A Japlish word. The Japanese love adapting English words. No Pants."

"You mean she's been working without knickers?" Ruby asked, delighted and shocked at the idea.

Kaoru rose from the pile of bodies with a roar. "You monster," he shrieked. You left me because I wanted things you thought were . . . were . . . And now you work, exposing yourself to all in a *nopan*?" he charged at her and she fell back before his anger.

He leaped at her, ripping at her clothes until she was

fully naked. The others looked upon in bemusement. It was clear no damage was really intended. Though the driver's arms were flailing, the length of his erect shiny prick kept on getting in the way. He pushed her to the floor then gripped her ankles and pulled them apart. The sight and smell of her golden fuzz greeted him. For a moment he stared down at her delightfully displayed vista, and then Kaoru gave vent to an animal-like howl. He pulled at her roughly and she peered at him with a mixture of fright and anticipation. Her crotch hairs, she knew, were moist again, glistening with the anticipation of pleasure.

Kaoru held Millicent's legs high in the air. For what seemed to her to take hours he simply stared downwards at the splayed juncture of her legs. Then, his cock jutting fiercely forward, he pushed her ankles towards her head. She knew she was entirely exposed to him, as well as to all the rest in the room. She dared not look around, but the feel of so many eyes on her was as exciting as the knowledge that the man staring so freely at her was going to ravish her helpless body.

Kaoru peered down angrily at the soft jungle that awaited him. He could see the length of Millicent's softness, nestled in the golden curls which ran from her belly to well beyond the dimple of her rear hole, and from one thigh to the other. He knew that he wanted to throw himself between her legs, to munch and kiss, to browse in the full musky meadow between her thighs. But the thought of the others who must have been there enraged him further. He drove himself angrily forward, penetrating her soft cunt with his entire weight. She gave before him, her insides so wet he fancied he could hear the 'splat' of his flesh meeting hers.

Millicent could barely restrain her cry as the sword of flesh penetrated her ass viciously. She had been anticipating it for days, had in fact almost given in to the owner of the Nopan from sheer desire. Kaoru's weight on her counted as nothing, nor did his terrible stare compared with the pleasure and joy she felt at the penetration of her flesh by him, and not by another.

Kaoru ground his hips into hers, attempting to subdue and be subdued by Millicent's willing flesh. His cock pounded away, his anger gradually giving way to a loving lust that the sight, and more importantly the feel, of her fur brought to him. The other three women were accomplished and pleasing, but he knew that for him the greatest pleasure would lie in Millicent's hirsute crotch. He wallowed in the feeling, his hands sunk into her bush, pulling at the soft hairs, stroking their matted surface, longing to touch it with his tongue, his cock, his fingers all at the same time. Millicent was gasping underneath him. Her strong rather crooked teeth were showing and her hands were pressing into him. She had grown her nails since they had last been together and she now drew red marks across his shoulders, digging them hard into his skin. He pulled out of her, yielding to the temptation of the minute. Sliding his hands down her legs he raised them high into the air again. She looked at him reproachfully but waited patiently for his next move. His cock rolled in the meadow of her hair like an animal enjoying the grass. The feel—soft yet rough—was one he had dreamed of for weeks, ever since she had left him. Then with a convulsive heave he thrust into her once again. She cried out in passion and suddenly he found her arms contracting around him, her mouth searching for his as her orgasm burst a dam of frustration, love, and lust. His own desire for her rose to uncontrollable heights and his own balls, only parted emptied by his previous encounter, spurted worth with unleashed power as he shook her body onto to his.

He pulled back to examine his work. His white sperm had bubbled and seeped out from her channel. The lips were still slightly open, and as he watched, the last of her orgasmic contractions brought a fresh outwelling of the white gluey fluid from between the pink lips. They lay on her matted moist hairs, running down, coating the tiny crated that marked her rear entrance. For a moment he stared, entranced. His erection was still full, his lust and love undiminished by the first spurts of barely felt pleasure. With a cry he sank himself down into the bowl of her thighs, piercing her virgin flesh.

Millicent cried out in outrage as he slipped forward from above her. The invasion of her posterior was something she had denied, and yet knew it was to come. At first her instinct was to object, to run, to deny this massive invasion of herself. Then in a flash she remembered her first time with Donald. He too had invaded her, in a way and place she had not known was possible. "Carnal knowledge" until the night of her marriage was but a phrase, but as his maleness tore into the membrane of her maidenhead *down there,* suddenly she *knew.* This time though, she knew as well that it was enjoyable, that it was what she wanted, and she surrendered to the invasion, knowing that the pain would pass. With her internal surrender came a relaxation of her muscles, and suddenly the urgent staff that was butting at the muscles of her rear became the pleasurable instrument that Kaoru had introduced to her in a snowy tunnel in the Japan Alps.

"Kaoruuu!" she cried out, and her hands went around his back, pulling him to her urgently, forcing still more of his flesh into hers.

The sun was high overhead. Tokyo was as muggy as only a large city can be. The traffic sounds were muted. Andy was lazily tending to his latest interest: raising chrysanthemums. He had hidden hopes of displaying the classical arrangements at the neighborhood show in the Fall. Jim, scratching his bare leg comfortably and sipping at his beer, was working the crossword puzzle. Snowdrifts of Sunday newspapers lay around him on the *engawa.*

"Think its going to get any better?" Jim asked.

Without turning his head, Andy laughed, then wiped his forehead. "How could it? I just hope it goes along as it is."

"You mean with Ruby and all."

"Yep. Not to mention Hsi-wen. We've got big plans, that girl and I."

"Yeah. Best damn whorehouse franchise in the world. SuccSex to go."

"Something like that," Andy agreed.

"Sure the world is ready for that?" Jim inquired, picking up the paper again.

"Wake up man. This *is* the world. Those other pieces, across the ocean and on the other side of the continent? They're just the provinces."

The tiny chrysanthemum heads, three to a stalk, nodded in agreement.